SONGBIRD
JAX DIAMOND MYSTERIES

SONGBIRD

Jax Diamond Mysteries

Book 1

Gail Meath

Book Trailer: https://youtu.be/OcECJje7Crc

Website: https://www.gailmeath.com

A DEDICATION AND THANK YOU TO:

Jim, my husband, has never read any of my books, yet he helped me with some very clever ideas when I was stumped.

Ryan Murphy, our grandson, knows everything there is to know about the mechanics of cars, no matter the model, make, or how old they are. And I am going to especially need his help in the second book of the series.

Bonnie DeMoss, Editor

Cover Design by Sheri McGathy

TABLE OF CONTENTS

1

New York City
1923

Tuesday, May 29

Sam tossed his fork back onto the plate. He shifted uncomfortably in his seat, moved the brass desk lamp a few inches closer, and continued reading the final draft of his new musical.

He had to admit that he'd written a brilliant play, superior to any production on Broadway thus far. He'd spent three months working on it, day and night. Ever since he heard *her* sing. At that moment his own creativity seemed to burst alive and the ideas kept flowing so quickly, he couldn't stop writing until he finished the script. After editing it for the hundredth time, he knew this play would not only prove extremely profitable for the theater owner and the talented performer who had inspired him, but it would also boost his career to amazing heights. After all, no other composer had ever written an entire musical from start to finish, foregoing the lyricist and book writer.

He looked at the telephone beside him. He wondered why his wife had made a rare appearance at the Ambassador this afternoon. She never ventured to the theater unless she was dressed to the nines for a night out on the town, usually without him. As he'd worked with the performers on stage, he caught a glimpse of her standing by the entranceway, but she quickly disappeared out the door.

He should phone her, he supposed, but he wasn't up to dealing with his personal problems tonight, not when he was so close to finishing this play. He'd already been paid a hefty advance from the owner of the Globe Theater. As soon as they discussed a production start date at their meeting tomorrow morning, he would face what awaited him at home.

A fat drop of sweat dripped from his brow and splattered across the page in front of him. Then another. He cursed out loud, snatched the cloth napkin, and dragged it across his forehead. He'd forgotten to open the window, which was the first thing he habitually did when he came to this hellhole of an apartment. This tiny room was always hotter than blazes no matter the weather outside.

He stood up to open the window, but the room took a quick spin around him, and he stumbled backward against the desk. With a puzzled frown, he snatched the arm of his chair and eased himself back into it. He took off his suit jacket and necktie and tossed them aside. He sat there for a moment, breathing slowly and deeply to clear his head. Within a few minutes, the dizziness subsided, so he went back to reading the script.

But when he turned the page, he noticed his hand was trembling. He stared at his fingers and became almost mesmerized by them. A sharp prickly sensation spread through each one from tip to base before they went numb altogether as if he'd kept his hand in an awkward position too long, and it fell asleep. He lifted his arm, flapped his hand in the air, and wiggled his fingers around to get the blood flowing again. The numbness soon disappeared.

With the same bewildered scowl, he looked up at the pendulum clock on the wall and squinted as the numbers appeared blurry. He removed his glasses and squeezed his eyes open and shut a few times. He'd been working too many hours. And the filthy ventilation and dim lighting in this room weren't helping. But even with his glasses back in place, the typewritten words on the manuscript became fuzzy. Then, they seemed to be dancing across the page on their own, picking up speed the harder he tried to focus on them.

He pushed his chair back in panic, wondering what the hell was happening to him, but he suddenly doubled over in agony as crushing bolts of pain shot through him from the pit of his stomach to his chest.

Frightened out of his wits, he tried focusing on the telephone while struggling to lift himself upright. But his arms had gone numb and were useless. Using the strength of his legs and the chair behind him, he thrust himself forward and slammed down face-first onto the mahogany desk. The two-hundred-page manuscript burst into the air like confetti while the dinner plate crashed to the floor.

As he lay there gasping for air, he gathered every ounce of strength he could muster, and what lucidity he had left, and slowly dragged his right arm up along the top of the desk to reach the telephone. Just as his fingertips touched the base, he heard the door creak open.

His light eyes rolled upwards then grew wide and horrified. He tried calling for help, but only a sick gurgling noise emerged from his throat before the room went dark.

2
Jax Diamond

Jax stepped out of his car, a burgundy jalopy he'd picked up for a couple of tens a few months ago. He leaned against it and folded his arms in front of him as he stared at the tenement house across the street, the second-floor window mid-way. Like all others, it remained dark and had been for hours. It was nearing three o'clock in the morning, and there wasn't a soul on the streets, although he knew of a few gin joints down the road that were open another hour.

"Stay put, Ace." He pulled a leftover rib bone out of his overcoat pocket and tossed it into the front seat of his car. The hundred-pound black and tan shepherd laid down and happily gnawed on it.

Jax made his way across the street. He tapped the front hood of the Fiat parked at the curb with his index finger and climbed up the few steps to the front door of the building. He glanced up beneath the brim of his brown fedora, then behind him before retrieving a pocketknife from his trousers. While holding the knife in one hand and the doorknob in the other, he carefully slipped the file into the latch and started jiggling both simultaneously. Within seconds he was able to push the latch bolt back, and he opened the door. He tucked his knife into his pocket and pulled out a small flashlight. After another glimpse around, he entered the building. He climbed the stairway to the second floor and made his way down the hall.

When he stood in front of the center room, he took a deep breath and knocked softly. "Mister Sanders?" The man didn't answer, so he turned the doorknob and the wooden door slowly swung open. After shining the light around the entire room, he saw the body sprawled lifelessly across the desk. He tipped his hat off his forehead and placed his hands on his hips beneath his overcoat.

"Swell..."

After another moment, he stepped inside and was caught not only by the sweltering temperature of the room but by the putrid stench of vomit and whatever else that stink was. He pulled out a beige handkerchief from his suit pocket, used it to close the door behind him, then quickly covered his mouth and nose for a few minutes until he could handle the smell. He turned the desk lamp on and got a good look at the body. And he cursed himself for waiting so long.

He'd been trailing the man for a couple of weeks now. It had been three hours since the light went off in this room just before midnight, which usually meant Sanders was heading out. It was just plain stupid on his part for assuming the man had fallen asleep. Sanders never wavered from his strict routine.

Jax went over to the window and took a quick look outside before pulling the striped curtain shut. When he turned around, he noticed the man's necktie and suit jacket lying on the floor beside the wooden chair that had tipped over on its side. He picked up the jacket to check the pockets and noticed a flower neatly pinned to the left lapel. A white lily. He stared at it, deep in thought, then laid the jacket down on the floor.

He continued scanning the rest of the room. Sanders had

left the theater at exactly five o'clock. Habitually, he carried his black metal lunch pail with his dinner that had been delivered to him at the theater from a high-class joint on Fifty-Fifth Street. He drove four and a half miles and arrived at the apartment ten minutes later. But there wasn't any sign of the man's dinner, the paper containers his meal was packed in, silverware, or a thermos. Even his lunch pail was missing.

Jax went back to the desk, lifted the phone receiver with his handkerchief, and dialed the number. "You'd better get over here, Murph. I'm at the flophouse on the corner of Essex and Canal Street on the Lower East Side. Second floor. There's a dead body. Yes, he's dead. No, I didn't touch anything." And he hung up.

He knew Sergeant Tim Murphy and his eager police crew would be here in a flash. They always were after he called as though they were just sitting by the phone waiting until he stumbled upon something, knowing he would eventually. And while most of the cops didn't like him, Murph did. They've been close pals the past five years and now, they were unofficial partners. Although Murph hated it when he made that reference, which he did as often as he could just to needle him.

Jax opened the top drawer of the desk, but it merely held writing utensils, a couple of erasers, spools of typewriter ribbon, and wire clips. In the second drawer, he saw a small piece of scrap paper lying on top of a stack of folders with the name *Louis Godfrey* written on it along with a telephone number. He tucked it into his pocket and flipped through the folders, but he found nothing of interest in them. Underneath those, there was a thick envelope with a wad of Benjamins totaling a thousand bucks inside. He shoved the bills back into the envelope, placed it on top of the folders, and closed the drawer.

He walked around to the front of the desk, moved his overcoat aside, and squatted to get a better look at the corpse. He cringed when he saw the greenish-brown spew around the man's mouth. "What the heck happened, Sanders? I've been right across the street the whole night."

The man's left arm hung limply over the side of the desk and his middle finger was bare. Yet, it still held the indentation and skin discoloration from a rather large ring. Jax searched the floor thinking it may have slid off, and he slowly ran his hand along the small space underneath the desk full length across. He touched something sharp and pulled it out. It was a broken piece of a ceramic plate a couple of inches wide imprinted with an eagle emblem. There wasn't any residue on it, so he dropped it into another pocket.

On the other side of the desk, he saw a wastebasket and carefully rummaged through it, but all he found were a few crumpled sheets of paper. He stuffed those into his overcoat pocket.

The man's death appeared routine, heart failure, or some other disgusting fatal condition since he'd obviously gotten physically ill. And there wasn't any trace of blood or visible marks on him suggesting strangulation. But he wasn't about to jump to any conclusions yet. Not when he knew Sam Sanders was married, lived in Upper Manhattan, and had paid for six months' rent in advance for this crappy apartment.

Three weeks ago, the man's wife had called him, and they met for coffee. She told him that her husband claimed to be working late at the theater a few days a week. But the previous night when she tried to get ahold of him, she was told that he'd left the theater hours ago. She suspected he was having an affair, and she wanted Jax to trail him. So, for a sizeable fee, he agreed, and right off, he discovered Sam Sanders' secret apartment.

The trouble was, until last night no one except the other tenants, with or without friends, had entered or left the building. At least not during his frequent observations from his car parked across the street. He couldn't find any evidence that Sanders was unfaithful to his wife. Even last night was questionable. He had gotten a good look at the beautiful young woman through his binoculars as she walked up the street, then waited outside until Sanders opened the door for her at five thirty-five. She didn't stay long, barely twenty minutes, which he guessed might be plenty of time for some lovers.

Yet, Sanders didn't close the curtains after she entered his apartment, and this room was barely big enough to fit the man's desk and chair, let alone provide anyone enjoyment. No fold-out bed, cot, blanket, or anything in the form of comfort.

He shrugged his shoulders. But maybe that was just him.

He heard two cars pull up outside and made his way back into the hall to wait for Tim and his crew. "Sorry about getting you up and out so early, Murph," he greeted as Tim headed down the hallway with two other officers following along. "The man's name is Sam Sanders. He's a playwright for the Ambassador theater."

"After we have a look around, you and I need to chat." Tim reached over and gave Jax's necktie a tug to straighten it out. Then, he headed inside the room, but he stopped short, caught by the stench. He swore under his breath and cleared his throat a few times before continuing.

Officer Collins followed along. "Don't you ever sleep, Diamond?"

"Someone needs to stay up and do your job, Stan."

He glared at Jax as he entered the apartment.

"Where there's trouble, Detective Diamond is never far away," Officer Moriarty chortled.

Jax cracked up laughing and slapped him on the back. "You slay me, Butch! I'll have to jot that one down."

Butch scowled at him and joined the others.

Jax waited in the hall, watching them from the doorway as they studied the body and inspected the room. Tim opened the desk drawers and found the envelope. He handed it to Stan and told him to turn it over to the desk clerk at the station. Finally, he reached down and picked up the jacket. Tim stood there quietly for a moment before pulling the chair upright and draping the jacket over the back of it.

"Looks like the poor sap died from a heart attack," Stan said.

Tim shuffled him and Butch back into the hallway. "I'll wait here for the coroner. Why don't you both head back to the station? Don't lose that money on your way over there, Stan," he added with a snicker. Once they were out of earshot, he turned to Jax. "There had to be nearly a grand in his drawer."

"What do you make of that lily pinned to his jacket? Reminds me of the Broadway Butterfly murder case we had a couple of months ago."

Tim sighed irritably. "She had a flower in her hair, which isn't unusual for some women."

"Yeah, but it was a lily, just like the one on Sanders' jacket. And that other case is still unsolved."

"Kitty Cooper was a victim of a robbery gone wrong, Jax. Sanders had a wad of dough in his drawer. Untouched. Besides, his death looks to be from natural causes. Now would be the perfect time to tell me why you're here."

"As usual, I'm on an assignment, Murph. Sanders arrived here just after five o'clock, and I've been sitting in my car across the street the whole time. I didn't see anything suspicious. Wish I could tell you more, but you know, client confidentiality and all."

"Yeah, I know. How'd you get in the building? The door downstairs was locked."

Jax didn't miss a beat. "One of the other tenants got home just in time to let me in."

"Yeah, sure. What's Sanders, about late thirties, early forties?"

"Thirty-eight last February. He and his wife, Patricia, live at sixteen Bleecker Street in Manhattan. That's his blue Fiat Torpedo parked out front. I wouldn't mind taking that baby for a spin."

"Why does he have a separate apartment?"

Jax remained silent.

"Any kids?"

"Nope."

"Well, that makes it a little easier when I inform his wife. I hate when kids are involved, having two of my own."

"Oh, that reminds me, Murph." Jax reached into his back pocket. "Here are four tickets to the Yankees game against the

Red Sox on Saturday afternoon. I've got one for myself, so tell little Petey and Lizzie that I'll see them there."

"Three would have been enough. You know Carla hates baseball."

"Baloney. She loves baseball! I think she has a crush on Lou Gehrig."

Tim rolled his eyes and looked at the body inside the room again. "Not a pretty way to go, was it?"

"Good evening, boys," Joe Marsh, the coroner, said as he joined them. "Or rather, good morning. My assistants are carrying the stretcher up."

"It looks like a heart attack, Joe," Tim told him. "His name is Samuel Sanders."

Joe nodded, went into the room, and set his black bag on the floor. A half-hour later, he finished his examination and joined Tim and Jax in the hallway while the other two men carried the body downstairs. "It's difficult for me to determine the time of death. A few hours would be my guess."

"Natural causes, Joe?" Jax asked.

"Looks like it, but Doctor Norris will want to examine him. Tim, have the man's doctor send his medical files over as soon as you can." He bid them good morning and left.

"There you have it, Jax," Tim said. "Cut and dried. Just the way I like it." But he saw the smirk on Jax's face. "You're thinking something else happened here, aren't you?"

"It's not up to me, Murph. Doctor Norris is the expert. Let me know what he finds out. I've been working around the clock the past few weeks, and I need to get some sleep." And he headed off.

"Jax!" Tim yelled after him. "You *will* fill me in on the rest of this and give me whatever you took from the room after you get a good look at it, right?"

He threw his hand up in a wave. "I always do, Murph."

3
Laura Graystone

Wednesday, May 30

The sold-out crowd in the Ambassador Theater burst to their feet in a standing ovation before the stage performers finished the grand finale of the show's one-hundredth performance. Their applause roared like thunder, drowning the orchestra, vibrating the wooden floors, and sending a colorful display of lights dancing across the ceiling from the quivering chandelier overhead. The house manager, ushers, and concession personnel who had inconspicuously gathered at the back of the theater joined in. Even Missus Ashworth, the wealthy widow of a real estate magnate, stood applauding in the front row.

Forty-five minutes later, the heavy crimson drapes were slowly drawn upwards again for the seventeenth curtain call, the most ever recorded at the theater. The entire cast of the musical, *Blossom Time*, lined the stage, smiling and holding hands, thrilled that their performance was such a success. Then, they began clapping in acknowledgment and gratitude to the orchestra, conductor, and stage crew.

George Mitchell leaned down and whispered to Laura, who stood beside him in the center of the stage. She shook her head, but he pulled her forward, and with their hands still entwined, he lifted hers in special acknowledgment of her performance. Dozens of long-stem red roses flew through the air and landed on stage at Laura's feet as the crowd chanted, "Songbird! Songbird!"

Laura Graystone was new to Broadway, which was evident by the sparkle of surprise in her hazel eyes and the humble pink fluster on her cheeks as she waved to her fans. At twenty-three years old, she had made her debut with the Follies only last January, and the following day, the New York Times had dubbed her 'Songbird' in their raving review. She couldn't have been happier or more flattered. Two months later, she was offered the lead in this production, replacing the original actress, and it was her dream come true.

She blew kisses to the cheering audience. Then, she turned towards Missus Ashworth, who had made her debut possible, and gracefully dipped in a formal curtsy. Everyone kept shouting her nickname, and she couldn't help but laugh in disbelief. George told her that she deserved every bit of their adoration and offered his arm to escort her back into line with the others. Finally, the curtains closed, and the cast dispersed.

Laura made a point of circling around backstage to thank as many of the cast and crew in person as she could. When she saw Mister Beacham, the surly old piano player, she hurried over to thank him.

He tucked his spectacles into his shirt pocket and stretched his chubby arms wide to embrace her. "Bravo, my dear."

"Thank you, Mister Beacham," she said, hugging him tightly. "I don't know what I would do without you. That A-chord always throws me off."

"It is you who guides me there. I have never heard such a beautiful and powerful voice from such a petite young woman."

"You are too kind. The cast is having a small celebration at Sardis this evening. Will you be coming?" With his nod, she quickly kissed his cheek and headed for her dressing room.

Her assistant, Annie, clasped her hands in a joyous greeting. "What a beautiful performance, Miss Laura! So quickly you have become a huge star."

"It sounds scarier when you say it aloud, Annie. I doubt I will ever get used to the bright lights and attention. Will you help me out of this costume? This satin romper is so tight I can barely breathe. I'm surprised I didn't split a seam during the dance moves."

Annie unbuttoned the back of her outfit. "I readied your ivory satin gown and silver t-straps for the celebration tonight."

"Thank you, Annie. I'm exhausted but I should attend for a little while. Did you see Missus Ashworth and her son in the front row? I can't believe they attended tonight. It was such a surprise."

"Do not give them too much credit," Annie complained. "I have worked for the family a long time, and they never put themselves out unless it benefits them."

Laura couldn't help but smile. As little as Annie was, barely reaching her chin, and a typical doting grandmother of six, she was a bold one, too, who never hid her true feelings. "Well, I am grateful to them for hiring you to assist me."

"I am thankful for that as well. You are a breath of fresh air after working for that nasty Kitty Cooper."

"Annie! It's bad luck to speak ill of the dead."

"She was not a nice person," Annie grumbled under her breath, then she quickly changed the subject. "Did you see all the lovely floral arrangements that were sent to you?"

Laura glanced over and saw the bouquets filling the far side of the room. "They're beautiful." And she disappeared behind the dressing screen.

"The Garthfields sent pink peonies," Annie told her. "The carnations are from Mister and Missus Farnham. Your mother sent a lovely bouquet of roses."

"She did? How sweet of her."

"The rest are from your many fans. And the Ashworths, of course."

Laura hesitated. "I see someone sent a single white flower. Do you know who it's from?"

"It did not come with a card."

Laura flung the misty rose romper over the top of the screen. "Remind me to send everyone a thank-you note, will you?" Just as she spoke, someone knocked on the door, and she quickly peeked out from behind the screen. "Don't let anyone in until I'm finished dressing."

Annie nodded and hurried to the door, but after she opened it, she lost her smile. "May I help you?"

"Good evening, ma'am. My name is Detective Diamond." He towered over her and scanned the room. "I'd like to chat with Miss Graystone for a few minutes."

She frowned and partially closed the door to block his view. "She is busy. You will have to come back later."

"I see. Could you at least let her know that I'd like to speak with her? It's important..." But she slammed the door in his face.

Laura sat down at the vanity to fix her hair. "Who was it, Annie?"

"Some man claiming to be a detective," she replied. "He looks like a ragamuffin to me. His hair is as unruly as his wrinkled brown suit, as though he just climbed out of bed. Apparently, he cares nothing about his appearance."

Laura laughed at her. "You're far too critical. You probably should let him in."

"And you are too trusting." But she slowly made her way to the door and opened it. Without saying a word and looking none too happy, she motioned for him to come inside.

"Thank you, Ma'am." He entered the room, smiling and glancing around in awe.

Laura stood up to greet him and tried not to giggle since Annie's description of him couldn't have been more accurate. His unkempt blonde hair spilled to his forehead, his suit was a wrinkled mess, and his crooked necktie was loose and hanging down the front of him nearly sideways. Yet, he was handsome, too, tall with penetrating blue eyes, clean-shaven, and a single dimple as he smiled.

Finally, his focus settled on her. "I'm a big fan of yours, Miss

Graystone."

"Thank you." But she lost his attention again as he continued looking around the room. "You wanted to talk to me?"

"Yes, I did," he replied, grinning. "My name is Jax Diamond, a private detective. I'm getting a real kick out of meeting you. I haven't had a chance to see any of your shows, but I read about you in the paper, and they say you're pretty amazing."

"Thank you again."

He pulled a notepad and pencil from his jacket pocket. "I need to ask you a few questions if you don't mind."

"I don't mind," she replied impatiently, wondering when he would get the point.

He studied his pad. "Did you visit Mister Samuel Sanders at his apartment on Canal Street last evening?"

"Yes, I did. Is something wrong?"

"I'd say so. He's dead."

"Oh." She fell back into her chair, and Annie rushed to her side.

"Sorry Miss Graystone. I assumed you had heard about it since the theater owners were notified earlier today."

"What happened to him?"

"Seems he had a heart attack during the night. I'm helping the medical examiner pin down the time of death. How well did you know Mister Sanders?"

It took her a minute to compose herself. "He wrote the script for this show and worked closely with all of us, the production company and the performers."

"Did you also meet Mister Sanders for dinner last Wednesday at..." He stared at his notepad and struggled, "Lag...a..."

"*L'Aiglon's*," she corrected. "It's a French restaurant."

His grin widened. "Right..."

"I met him there, but I didn't stay for dinner. I had a cab waiting for me and went directly back to my flat." But he kept watching her as though waiting for her to elaborate. "It pertained to my career if that's what you're fishing for."

"Did you leave alone?"

"Yes, I was alone, Detective," she replied. "Mister Sanders was still in the restaurant."

"About what time did you arrive at his apartment last night?" he asked, poising his pencil so he could write down this information, too.

She tried to think, but he was making her nervous now. "He sent me a note during rehearsal asking me to come to his apartment at five-thirty, so it was about that time."

"Did you go there by yourself?"

Her nervousness turned indignant. "Yes, Detective. *Again*, I was alone. It was regarding a business opportunity, so I saw no need for someone to accompany me."

"I just thought...well, it's kind of a rough neighborhood for a young lady traveling alone."

"It was daylight, not the dead of night."

He kept his eyes on her. "Did you know Mister Sanders had a wife?"

Annie moved forward angrily, but Laura held her back. "It's all right, Annie." She didn't like the question or his tone either. She stood up to face him. "Yes, I know he was married. What are you implying, Detective?"

"Look, Miss Graystone, these are all just routine questions I need to ask. Please don't take offense." Without skipping a beat, he asked, "What time did you leave his apartment last night?"

"I was there less than half an hour. I found out the front door is always locked, and the landlord was gracious enough to open it for me when I left. I'm sure he can confirm the time."

"He said the same thing," Jax replied as he wrote the information down.

She didn't like this man at all! First, he pretends to be a fan of hers then he makes indecent implications and asks her questions that have already been answered?

Jax wandered to the other side of the room to look at the floral arrangements. "You have a lot of fans."

"If there isn't anything else, I need to finish getting ready." She spoke firmly, hoping he would leave, but he lingered there, reading the cards tucked within the flowers. "Detective?"

Finally, he made his way towards the door. "Thank you for your time. It was a real pleasure meeting you." But just before the door closed, he stopped and looked over at the arrangements again. "I see someone sent you a gardenia. Are you partial to those flowers, Miss Graystone?"

She frowned at him. "Is that one of your routine questions?"

"No," he chuckled. "They're my mother's favorite. They have a very special meaning, you know. Looks like you have a secret admirer. Have a good evening, ladies." And he shut the door behind him.

Annie wrapped an arm around her. "This must be very upsetting for you, Miss Laura, and that rude detective was not very sympathetic."

"I'm fine, Annie, but I don't understand. If the Ashworths knew about this earlier today, why weren't we told of it?"

"Undoubtedly, they did not want to upset anyone and lose the profits for tonight's performance."

She was beginning to agree with Annie about their employers. "It's late. Why don't you go home to your family? I'm not up to celebrating anymore, and I'll be leaving soon, too."

But Laura sat at the vanity long after Annie left, staring into the mirror as she brushed her chestnut-colored bob. A thousand different thoughts were flying around in her head. And they all landed on Mister Sanders.

He seemed too young and healthy to have had a heart attack, although it happened, she supposed. The man obviously worked long hours. She remembered her father being overwhelmed and under a lot of stress when he worked too many hours. Ill health wasn't the cause of his death, but his heavy workload had taken quite a toll on him.

She grabbed her handbag, pulled out the manila folder, and flipped through the pages. She felt horribly callous, but she couldn't stop thinking about the new script that Mister Sanders had written. He'd told her that he wrote it specifically with her in mind for the starring role and had given her a copy of the music score last evening. Since she had merely replaced Kitty Cooper, the original actress in this musical, Mister Sanders' new play would have been a tremendous break for her.

He had even asked for her thoughts on the script after she looked it over. She was a greenhorn, as they say, a newcomer, an amateur. No one ever asked her for her opinion, and she certainly never expected anyone to, but Mister Sanders had seemed genuinely interested in her opinion. She couldn't help but wonder what would happen to the new script now.

Detective Diamond popped into her mind, and she shoved the folder back into her bag. The man was rude and insensitive, and she resented his implications about her meetings with Mister Sanders, as though he didn't believe they were strictly business matters. He even went as far as to question her about things that he already knew were true. Testing her as though she were a suspect in a crime.

Which raised another question. Why was a private detective investigating a death caused by a heart attack anyway?

With that on her mind, she glanced over at the single white gardenia within the crowd of bouquets, recalling the night she had received the first one. And her thoughts stopped there.

4
The Music Score

Thursday, May 31

"I'm not sure if he was a nitwit or just pretending to be one." Laura didn't even try to hide the cutting tone in her voice as she and Jeanie, her best friend, had coffee together at the neighborhood diner the next morning.

Jeanie laughed at her while she ate her soft-boiled egg. "That detective really got under your skin, didn't he? It takes a lot to get you riled up."

"I don't understand why he bothered asking me any questions. He already knew all the answers. And he kept writing everything down in that stupid notepad of his. He even implied something was going on between Mister Sanders and me. That's what made me so angry."

Jeanie rested her chin in her hand. "So, he was good-looking, huh?"

Laura shook her head. "That's all you think about, isn't it?"

"Mostly..."

"Robert Ashworth called me this morning. He said they decided to cancel our performances this weekend out of respect for Mister Sanders."

"Well, that was thoughtful, but no work, no pay."

"He also told me that his mother wants me to ride with them

to the funeral tomorrow morning. I hadn't planned on going, but he caught me off guard, and I couldn't think of an excuse to get out of it. Jeanie, please come with me."

She grabbed the salt-shaker and sprinkled more on her egg. "I can't, Laura. I have practice with the Follies from eight until noon." She set the shaker down, but it tipped over on its side, and a few grains of salt spilled on the table. She looked up at Laura. "I know. I know. Toss some over my left shoulder otherwise, I'll have bad luck all day." And she went through the motions. "What's with you and Robert Ashworth anyway? Are the two of you getting tight?"

"Of course not! I'm one of their employees."

"Well, if the two of you did get together just think of all the clothes and shoes you could buy. His mother owns half the city. What I wouldn't do to marry a wealthy man and live off him the rest of my life."

"Gold digger," Laura laughed. "Besides, I think Missus Ashworth would faint on the spot if her son ever got involved with a stage performer."

Jeanie leaned closer and lowered her voice. "Last winter, rumors were flying around that he was seeing Kitty Cooper on the sly. Now *she* was a gold digger and a real bearcat to boot. Of course, that was before..."

"Good morning, girls!" Margie called out as she balanced her cup of coffee and bagel and had a stack of newspapers under her arm. "What a beautiful day."

"Well, you're all bright-eyed and bushy-tailed this morning," Jeanie said.

"I have a good reason. I got that part that I auditioned for last week. With *Miss Songbird* out of the way, I was a shoo-in."

Laura lost her smile. "Are you still upset with me, Margie? I'm sure Missus Ashworth pulled strings to get me the part. That's the only reason the director chose me over you."

"Aw, honey..." She leaned over and pecked Laura on the cheek. "I was just kidding. You're perfect for that part. Here, I bought a few newspapers for you on my way over. You probably already saw your reviews from last night's performance, but I thought you'd like extra copies." She sat down and dropped the papers in front of her.

Laura spotted a picture of Samuel Sanders on the front page, pulled it closer, and started reading the article. "I forgot all about them..."

"How could you forget? You were a smash, of course. The audience loved you."

Jeanie leaned over Laura's shoulder. "Does it say how he died?"

"Are you reading about the playwright?" Margie asked. "That's a crying shame,
isn't it? He was a talented composer."

"It *was* a heart attack," Laura said thoughtfully. "I saw Mister Sanders the night he died. He left me a note asking me to meet him, and he looked perfectly healthy."

"What?" Jeanie practically fell out of her seat. "No wonder that cute detective jumped to the conclusion that something more was going on between the two of you."

"It wasn't anything like that, Jeanie," Laura defended. "Mister Sanders just wanted to talk to me about his new script again, the one I told you about last week."

Margie snatched her hand. "What cute detective? C'mon, doll, fill me in on all the gooey details."

"Last night, a private detective came to my dressing room to question me about Mister Sanders. It still doesn't make sense why he would be snooping around asking personal questions if the poor man died of ill health."

"The gumshoes in the books I've read are always digging around even after an investigation is over with," Jeanie chuckled. "That's what makes them so good. They usually come across a piece of evidence that the police overlooked."

Laura read the paper again. "The article says that Mister Sanders and his wife live in Manhattan. I wonder what he was doing with a separate apartment on the Lower East Side?"

Margie laughed. "I'll tell you what he was doing. What every married man in the city does when they get bored. Fool around, that's what. You're such a bluenose, Laura. I grew up in Brooklyn, and your tiny town of Millbury is a far cry from here."

Jeanie nudged Margie. "I'm from Millbury, too, and we're not backwoods. But I agree that having his own apartment is pretty suspicious."

"That's not why he wanted to meet with me!" Laura spouted indignantly.

"Okay, doll, if you say so," Margie kidded, patting her hand.

"You're getting yourself riled up over nothing," Jeanie told her. "The man died of a bad heart. It's not like he was murdered or anything."

Jeanie's words didn't make her feel any better. "Well, that detective was fishing around for something. And now I'm trapped into going with the Ashworths to the funeral tomorrow. They're always so depressing even when you don't know the person well. Can you go with me, Margie? Please?"

"Not on your life, honey."

Laura let out a heavy sigh. "I owe Missus Ashworth a lot, but I barely knew Mister Sanders. And the thought of going to another funeral..."

"No favor is without its cost," Margie quipped.

As Laura headed back to her apartment, Margie's last statement hounded her. Missus Ashworth was a millionaire, owning acres of real estate in the city, plus owning the Ambassador and several department stores. She lived in an enormous mansion that spread across an entire block on Fifth Avenue. And she was never seen in public without her priceless collection of diamonds and pearls adorning her neck and wrists.

Last Christmas, her personal advisor happened to see Laura's performance at the Whalom Playhouse back in Millbury. He'd made a quick call and before she knew it, she was traveling with him on a train to the city for an audition with the Ziegfeld Follies.

Yet, Missus Ashworth's very generous favors were not without their cost. After she arrived in the city, she had nowhere to stay. So, she lived with the woman and her son for a week before moving into the apartment down the hall from Jeanie and Margie's. Whenever the woman snapped her fingers, everyone within hearing distance was expected to jump. Including her. And Missus Ashworth's constant demands drove her crazy. She didn't know how Robert put up with it.

Laura stopped walking. There was something else plaguing her, too. The music score in her handbag. She suddenly changed her mind about going back to her apartment. She hurried across the street to catch the Manhattan Trolley that traveled from Brooklyn to the theater district on Broadway. She knew it was a moot point now, but she was aching to hear the tunes that Mister Sanders had written. It was such an honor that he'd had her in mind when writing it.

She got off the trolley on West Forty-Ninth Street and walked down the alley beside the Ambassador Theater. Even though all performances had been canceled for the weekend, she knew at least a few of the maintenance crew would be inside. She slipped through the back door and tiptoed up the stairs. When she reached the wings, she stood there a moment, gathering her nerve.

She eyed the mahogany upright piano at the rear of the stage. Mister Beacham's piano. She started biting her bottom lip as she glanced around to see if anyone was wandering about. When all remained quiet, she made her way across the stage, pulled out the piano bench, and spread a few pages of the music score across the piano rack.

As soon as she started playing the first tune, the entire world slipped away. It was such a beautiful ballad she didn't even sing the words. She just hummed along, grasping the full essence of it. She played it again, and this time, she sang out loud without any concern that someone might hear. She couldn't help it as the words and music captivated her. Page after page, she sang every tune with her heart beating wildly. She became so engrossed in the songs she could almost imagine George Mitchell singing the alto with her for the two duets included. And she didn't stop until she had sung every tune to the end.

Then, she sat there staring at the musical notes, hypnotized by them and relishing in what could have been.

She heard applause and jumped to her feet. Mister Beacham and Jimmy, one of the stage crew, stood a distance away, smiling. Her face flushed with embarrassment. "I didn't know anyone else was listening."

"That was exquisite," Mister Beacham said as they joined her.

She quickly slid the music back into her handbag. "They're just a few pieces I happened upon. Nice to see you, Jimmy. I've been meaning to thank you for all you've done for us these past few months."

"I appreciate that, Miss Graystone. Glad to help."

Mister Beacham rested his hand on the young man's shoulder. "Jimmy, would you mind putting that crate in the music room for me?"

He nodded. "Sure thing. See you later, Miss Graystone!"

Mister Beacham waited until he was out of earshot, then looked at her. "Tell me, my dear, where did you come upon that music?"

She held her head down. "I can't say. I'm sorry."

He took his spectacles off. "They are from Sam's new musical, aren't they? He gave me a copy of the score last weekend and asked me not to breathe a word about it to anyone yet. But he was hoping that production would begin in a few months, and he wanted me to work closely with you if that were the case."

"He did?"

"Yes. I was anxious to hear those tunes, myself, and now that I have, they impressed me as much as they did you. Sam was an extraordinarily talented man. It is obvious that he wrote this script from the depths of his heart. Which is how you sing. It was a match made in heaven that ended too soon."

She hated to ask yet couldn't help herself. "Do you know if he gave a copy of the script to the theater director?"

"I wondered the same thing and spoke with Director Rosenberg about it. He was unaware Sam had written a new script, so I promised to give him my copy later this afternoon. With good reason, Sam had high hopes for this play. He deserves to have this final production on stage as a tribute to what a genius he truly was."

5
The Widow

The housemaid at the Sanders' apartment asked Jax to wait in the vestibule while she informed Patricia Sanders of his visit. He watched her walk down the hallway into the living area and knock on the double doors to an adjoining room. It was a large apartment from what Jax could see, with additional hallways to both his left and right. And it was expensively furnished judging from the two oil paintings, a three-foot-tall marble sculpture, and the longcase pendulum clock just in this small space.

Patricia Sanders opened the doors. After the housemaid spoke to her, she leaned forward slightly to get a look at him. Then, she quickly glanced behind her before whispering to the maid and closing the doors again. The housemaid returned to him and said that he needed to wait there for a few more minutes. It was exactly that by the time Patricia Sanders stepped out of the room and motioned for him to join her.

Appropriately, she was wearing a slender black gown with her blonde hair tied back in a tight bun. "I wasn't expecting you today, Detective," she said curtly. "It would have been far less tacky if you had waited until after the funeral to collect your payment." She spun around, went back into the room, and sat down on the rose-colored sofa. She opened the top drawer of the end table beside her and pulled out an envelope.

"My apologies, Missus Sanders," Jax replied. "I guess I need to brush up on my courtesy skills."

"Don't be flippant. Here." She tossed the envelope to him. "It's the amount we agreed upon even though you came up empty-handed. I trust that also covers the cost of your confidentiality?"

He studied her closely without replying, noting her brusque responses matched the lack of remorse on her face, exactly. There were no remnants of tears having been shed. No tissues close by in case they came without warning. No cherished photographs balancing on the fireplace mantel or anywhere in the room. And not one photo album in sight that she had pulled out of storage so she could immerse herself in treasured memories, which seemed customary for most couples when they lost their spouse.

The woman was obviously angry with him for showing up here unannounced, that much was clear. Even more apparent was the fact that someone else had been in this room with her when he arrived. Someone she didn't want him to know about since that person was hiding on the other side of a second door into the room. He could see the shadow of someone's shoes moving along the bottom.

"The officer who informed me of my husband's death said that you were the one who found him, Detective," Patricia said. "There wasn't anything suggesting foul play?"

Without being offered, Jax sat down in the wing-back chair and set his hat on the oriental rug at his feet. Then, he pulled out his notepad and flipped through it. "Your husband's whereabouts the past few weeks have been pretty routine, Missus Sanders. Monday through Thursdays like clockwork, he was at the theater from eight o'clock in the morning sharp until five o'clock. That's when he headed to the apartment on Canal Street, staying there anywhere between eight and midnight before coming directly home. There was only one night he swayed from that schedule and ate dinner at L'Aiglon's Restaurant before going to his apartment."

"And you're telling me that he didn't have any visitors?"

"No, Ma'am."

She stood up and wandered over to the casement windows. "Well, I still think he was having an affair. Why else would he rent that apartment? I'm sure it was someone from the theater, like that new singer. She's all Sam talked about lately."

"What singer?" he asked as he pulled a pencil from his vest pocket.

"Laura something-or-other."

"Did you ever see them together?"

"I never ventured to the theater during working hours." She turned around to face him. "Do the police know I hired you?"

"The topic hasn't come up yet."

"Well, hopefully, it remains between us since none of this matters any longer, does it? I'm rather tired, Detective. I'm sure you don't mind showing yourself out."

Jax tucked his notepad into his pocket, grabbed his hat, and stood up. He watched the woman collapse on the couch and drape her arm across her forehead as though utterly exhausted. But he wasn't buying it.

"I'm sorry for your loss." He started to leave, then poked his head back into the room. "Oh, one more question, Missus Sanders. Was your husband accustomed to wearing any jewelry or accessories, like a wristwatch or a ring? I want to make a note to ensure that all his valuables are returned to you."

"He wasn't one to fuss with his appearance, but he always wore his father's gold ring. There are diamonds set within the etchings, and it's worth a small fortune. So, yes, please make sure that is returned to me."

As Jax climbed down the front steps, he studied the elaborate flower gardens that skirted the perimeter of the building, noting the vast assortment. Then, he walked in front of Sam Sanders' Fiat, which now belonged to his wife, to cross the road. But his attention was again drawn to the shiny Rolls-Royce Silver Ghost parked not far up the street, one of the most expensive cars on the road. He'd noticed it when he arrived. He wondered now if it belonged to a wealthy tenant in the next building. Or the person hiding in the other room in Patricia Sanders' apartment.

He got into his car, yet he sat there for a minute. "So, why did the woman hire us, Ace?" He reached over to pet him. "And why continue to insist that her husband was having an affair after the poor sucker died? Especially if she was the one cheating on him?"

He'd been hired by a few wives and husbands who suspected their spouses were unfaithful. Usually, their purpose was to gather proof for divorce, since adultery, bigamy, or impotence were the only grounds available for a successful divorce these days. It seemed strange for someone to go to all the trouble and expense of hiring him when they were the guilty party.

Still, he didn't like leaving any stone unturned, and her accusations just gave him another idea. He started his car and headed back to the Lower East Side. When he stood in front of Sam Sanders' apartment building, he pounded on the door until the landlord finally opened it.

"What do you want?" the man snapped at him.

"I'm Detective Diamond. I just have a couple more questions for you about Mister Sanders then I'll get out of your hair."

"What questions?"

"I wondered if he had moved any furniture out of his apartment recently." The man eyed him suspiciously. "Sir, it's important."

"I do not keep tabs on every tenant, but they are each given a small storage space in the basement for additional belongings."

"Would you mind if I took a look at his? I could get a judge to sign a warrant, then have a bunch of police here to search the entire premises if you'd prefer."

The landlord grumbled and opened the door. He led the way through the hall and down the cellar stairs. To the left, there was a large room partitioned with sections of chicken wire separating each tenant's storage area. Midway, the landlord found Sanders' room number and pointed to it. Then, he stood there with his arms folded around his potbelly and his foot tapping impatiently.

But Jax noticed the small space was empty while most of the other stalls were crammed with items. He heaved a sigh and headed towards the stairway, but he came to an abrupt halt when he saw a back door on the far side of the adjoining room. "Do the tenants have a key to that door?"

"Certainly not," the man stated.

Jax wandered over to see if it was locked. He examined it for any signs of forced entry, but it was securely locked.

Within the hour, he was heading for Sunset Park in Brooklyn. He put his speculations aside for now and concentrated on his next stop, paying Louis Godfrey a visit, the man whose name he'd found in Sanders' drawer. He had called the number and spoke to a lovely woman named Dolores who sweetly told him that the man was an attorney.

After he pulled up to the curb, he entered the building and walked down the small hallway. When he reached the third door, he saw the man's name plate and entered the office. A young woman sat at the front desk. She was in her early twenties he'd guess, conservatively dressed, and wearing wire-framed eyeglasses. "Excuse me, is this Mister Godfrey's office?"

"Yes, sir. I'm Dolores."

He smiled at her. "My younger sister's name is Dolores. It's a beautiful name."

She blushed. "Thank you. How can I help you?"

"Would Mister Godfrey be available?"

"I'm sorry, but he has appointments out of the office all day. Did you want to leave a message for him?"

"Yes, if you don't mind." He dragged a chair over and sat beside her. "I think I spoke with you on the telephone yesterday. My name is Detective Jax Diamond. I'm investigating Samuel Sanders' death and I wondered..."

Her dark eyes grew wide. "My girlfriend just told me about the man's death this morning. Such a tragedy. Was he Patricia Sanders' husband?"

Her response surprised him. "Yes. Is she one of Mister Godfrey's clients?"

Dolores nodded.

"Do you know why she needed his services?"

Dolores hesitated. "I'm not at liberty to say, Detective Diamond."

He grinned at her. "Please, call me Jax." When she smiled coyly in return, he leaned closer. "Is that Chanel perfume you're wearing?"

She slid her glasses off. "Why, yes, it is. How did you know?"

"It was my sister's favorite, and you're just as pretty as she is."

Dolores giggled and batted her eyes at him.

"Tell me, Dolores, what types of legal issues does Mister Godfrey handle?"

She glanced around to make sure no one was listening. "Missus Sanders wanted to file for divorce. She even offered Louis...Mister Godfrey a generous sum of money to push it through. But he told her that she would need to provide solid proof of her husband's adultery before he could file."

"I see. Thank you, Dolores," Jax said as he stood up. "You have been most helpful. It was such a pleasure meeting you."

"Come by anytime," she replied sweetly as he walked out the door.

A few hours later, Jax sat at his kitchen table drinking a bottle of his homemade beer and waiting for the pot roast and spuds to finish cooking. He'd had a productive day. It made sense that Sam Sanders either knew about his wife's decision to divorce him since he had the lawyer's name and number in his drawer. Or he'd come upon the information and intended to speak with Louis Godfrey about it. He also knew that Patricia Sanders had been desperate for proof against her husband to obtain the divorce, which explained why she had hired him.

"But she lied to me, Ace. She's been to the theater during working hours. She was there the afternoon her husband died. She didn't see us tucked down that alley, and she wasn't there long, but she was there for sure. And right about the time, her husband's meal was delivered."

Finally, he went over to the small stove, pulled the roast out of the oven, and set a tin cover over it to let it rest for ten minutes or so. Meanwhile, he caramelized the carrots in the pot on the stove then skillfully carved the beef, slathered gravy over the meat and potatoes, and added a scoop of carrots to both servings. He set Ace's plate on the floor and sat back down at the table with his.

He straightened out the crumpled sheets of paper that he'd found in the waste basket at the apartment and looked them over. It was a portion of a handwritten music score. When he flipped to the second page, he noticed the title of the play was *Songbird.*

6
The Funeral

Friday, June 1

At eight-thirty the next morning, Laura flew down the stairs and out the front door of her apartment building. The funeral started in half an hour and Robert and his mother were waiting for her in their car out front. "I apologize for being late," she said as she struggled to climb into the retractable back seat.

"Tardiness is not a flattering quality, Laura," Missus Ashworth scolded.

"Yes, ma'am," she replied obediently.

As they drove to the church in lower Manhattan, she remained quiet. Robert did as well, while his mother complained about how early the funeral was since they apparently weren't supposed to begin until ten o'clock. Then, she began lecturing Robert about his own health, reminding him that his father had died of a heart attack, and he needed to take better care of himself.

"Please, mother. Let's not get into that again," Robert stated firmly.

"Suzanne told me that she overheard you arguing with Benjamin Hoffman on the telephone yesterday morning," Missus Ashworth persisted. "Why would you be discussing anything with him? He is the owner of the Globe and a competitor of ours."

"It was a misunderstanding. Nothing to concern yourself

with, Mother."

Laura slid deeper in her seat while Missus Ashworth stiffened in hers. The woman glared at her son while he kept his focus on the road straight ahead. "Do not patronize me, Robert. I may be getting on in years, but I still have full control of all finances and assets. I told you that I want to be kept abreast of any business dealings as well as any issues that arise."

"Yes, mother," Robert stated irritably.

The church service lasted an hour, and thankfully, all remained quiet in the car as they headed for the nearby cemetery. The minister began another sermon at the burial grounds, and it wasn't until then that Laura realized she didn't see Mister Beacham here or at the church, which seemed strange. When they spoke yesterday, it was obvious that he held the highest regard for Mister Sanders. He even referred to him by his first name, as though they knew each other well.

Yet now that she thought about it and glanced around again, she was the only theater employee who had attended the funeral.

That curiosity quickly fled when the service ended, and they paid their respects to the widow. Laura stood behind Robert and his mother while they spoke to Missus Sanders. After the two of them walked away, she offered her condolences and turned to leave.

But Missus Sanders snatched her arm. "I didn't catch your name."

"Laura Graystone. I'm one of the performers at the Ambassador Theater."

"Ah, yes, I've heard of you," the woman said, scowling. Finally, she released her grip.

Laura was frowning, herself, in confusion as she hurriedly caught up with Robert and his mother. She followed them to their vehicle, but she kept glancing behind her, wondering about the woman's reaction. That is until they reached the road. To make matters worse, Detective Diamond was leaning against an old burgundy Chevy parked at the curb. As soon as he saw them, he wandered over.

"Good morning," he greeted.

"What are you doing here, Detective Diamond?" Robert asked with as much annoyance as Laura felt.

"I didn't want to disturb anyone at the church, but I need to speak with Missus Sanders. Good morning, Miss Graystone."

She acknowledged him with a nod yet remained silent.

"Who is this man?" Missus Ashworth spouted.

"No one of importance Mother," Robert told her. "This isn't a suitable time, Detective. Missus Sanders has invited everyone to a private luncheon. At least give her this day to mourn the death of her husband."

Jax saw the procession surrounding the widow as they escorted her out of the cemetery. "I suppose it could wait."

Laura stared at Robert in disbelief. "We're going to a luncheon now?" She had been respectful enough to come to the funeral with them, but she never expected to spend her entire day engulfed in it! She didn't know what to do. How to get out of it. Her eyes darted back and forth now between both men, trying to decide the worst of two evils. "Mister Ashworth, I apologize, but I wasn't aware of a luncheon. I need to get back home. I have...another pressing commitment this afternoon." She quickly looked over Jax and dreaded her next words like the plague. "I hate to trouble you, Detective, but would you mind giving me a lift back to my apartment in Brooklyn?"

"We can drop you off, Laura," Robert told her.

"No, no," she said nervously. "It's too far out of your way." And if she rode with them, his mother would make her feel so guilty, she'd end up going to the luncheon anyway. "I'm sure the Detective doesn't mind."

"Of course not. Hop in," he replied jovially.

As she scurried over to his car, she heard Missus Ashworth calling to her. Laura shouted her thanks and waved to them. But when she reached the passenger side, she saw the large shepherd sitting in the seat and stopped short. Then, she slowly backed away. "Detective! I could use a hand here."

Jax walked over to her, laughing. "Ace, get in the back seat." And he opened the door for her. "He's harmless, Miss Graystone."

But she didn't budge. "I've heard that line before."

"Well, pick your poison," Jax told her. "Us or them."

She glared at him and slid into the front seat.

Jax shut her door and leaned down. "Ace, give the nice lady a kiss."

Before Laura could duck out of the way, Ace darted forward and swiped his tongue across her cheek. She burst out laughing and reached behind her to pet him.

Jax got into the driver's side, but he sat there for a few minutes.

"Is there a problem, Detective?" she asked.

"Nope." He started the car. "You don't have any other commitments this afternoon, do you, Miss Graystone? You said that to get out of going to lunch. I can always tell when someone is lying."

She set her handbag on the floor and relaxed in her seat. "I'm sure you can."

He put the car in first gear and headed off. "I was hoping for a private moment to talk with you."

"Do tell." At this point, she didn't even care. He'd just spared her an entire afternoon of uncomfortable mingling with Missus Ashworth and a crowd of people she didn't know. She took off her cloche hat and stuffed it into her handbag. The canvas top was rolled down, so she leaned back, took a few deep, refreshing breaths, and relished in the cool breeze against her face.

"I wanted to ask you about your meeting with Sam Sanders the other night."

"Detective, if the man had a heart attack as the newspaper said, why are you looking into the matter at all?"

"I have my reasons."

She turned towards him. "So, you want me to answer your questions, but you don't have to answer mine?"

He smiled. "Yeah, that's about right."

"Well then, I don't think I'm going to say another word. Not until you do."

She had successfully silenced him and was glad of it. But Ace started barking and she sat up. There was a black cat at the side of the road in front of them. As their car approached, the cat darted across the street. Laura squealed for Jax to stop, but the cat made it safely, and Jax continued driving.

"Oh, dear," Laura sighed.

"What's wrong?" he asked. "The cat's okay."

"It was a black cat."

"So?"

"It's bad luck when a black cat crosses your path," she told him.

"Hogwash," he chuckled. "That's an old wives' tale."

"Maybe so, but my mother always told me, it's better to be safe than sorry."

Jax smirked to himself. They drove several miles without another word until the car suddenly started spitting and sputtering. "Dang. Old Nellie is getting tired again." And the car came to a dead stop in the middle of the road.

Laura stared at him, waiting for him to make some sort of move. "We're just going to sit here?"

He shrugged his shoulders. "She usually gets going again after a few minutes. It happens now and then."

"Are you pulling my leg, Detective? Don't you know anything about automobiles?"

"Not much."

She swung the car door open, grumbling, "Next time a black cat crosses your path, turn around and go the other way. Shut the ignition off. Do you have any tools? A screwdriver, socket wrench, or anything along those lines?" But he just stared blankly at her. "How about some *rags*?"

"Sure. I should have some in the trunk."

She made her way to the front of the car, unlatched the hood, and pried it open. Impatiently, she waited for Jax, then she leaned over the engine. "Gads, it's filthy."

"What is?"

"The throttle. See? Right here. I can do a quick cleaning for now, but you should have a mechanic look at it soon. These Baby Grands are a sweet ride, but you need to keep up with regular maintenance. Especially at her age. Their innards tend to gobble up dirt and grime, then stall on you."

She finished wiping the valve assembly and intake pipe as best as she could, then she grabbed the last rag to clean the grease from her hands. "Luckily, I wore black today. Okay, try starting her up again." Jax got back into the car and turned the key. When the car rumbled smoothly, Laura gently closed the hood, tossed the dirty rags on the floor in the backseat, and got in.

"And exactly where did you learn how to do that, Miss Graystone?"

She turned a smug grin on him. "Answer my questions, Detective, and I'll answer yours. Quid pro quo, as they say."

"Excuse me?"

"Oh, for goodness sakes. Tit for tat, does that make better sense to you? You give me information, and I'll give you some." He looked at her like she had three heads. "Never mind. Just take me back to my apartment. I have the funny feeling you know the way."

Twenty minutes later, they parked in front of Laura's apartment building. Jax turned the car off and leaned back in his seat. "I'm not convinced it was a heart attack."

"I knew it," she whispered under her breath.

"There were a couple of things I found and some things I didn't find in Sanders' apartment that night that don't add up. I have a friend who is a sergeant on the police force, and I haven't said anything to him yet. He's always accusing me of making a mountain out of a molehill, so I wanted to check things out first in case I'm wrong. Does that fit in with your quid pro stuff?"

Proudly, she folded her arms in front of her. "Yes, I believe it does, Detective Diamond. What did you want to ask me?"

He pulled out his notepad and pencil. "You said that your meetings with Sam Sanders pertained to your career. How?"

"He'd written a new musical and...I was hoping he'd choose me for the lead."

He pointed the pencil at her. "Aha! You're lying again, Miss Graystone."

She glared at him. "How do you know?"

"Your pretty hazel eyes moved away from me as you spoke."

Now they rolled upwards in exasperation. "Okay, so he *chose* me for the lead in the play."

"That's better. What was the name of the play?"

"Oh, no, Detective. You need to give me an answer first. What did you find at his apartment that you're not sharing with the police?"

He looked straight ahead now. "Something in his wastebasket."

"Such as? And let me see those baby blues of yours, Detective."

He laughed. "Several sheets of paper. From what I could tell, the title of the play he was writing was Songbird. That's your nickname, isn't it?"

She lowered her head. "Yes. Mister Sanders approached me a few weeks ago and mentioned that he'd been working on the play. He asked me to meet him at L'Aiglon's to tell me more about it. The other night, he gave me a copy of the music score to look over. That's why I went to his apartment. It was a great honor having him write a musical for me, especially with his reputation."

"So, he wrote it *for* you?"

She snapped her head up. "With me in mind for the lead, I meant to say."

"Right. If he gave you a copy, then he still had the original?"

"He was reviewing it when I left his apartment."

Jax wrote that down. "Did he get along with everyone at the

theater?"

"Hold on. It's my turn. What *didn't* you find at the apartment? You said there were things you found and didn't find."

Jax hesitated, then flipped through his notepad. "He was carrying his dinner with him when he arrived at the apartment, but I couldn't find any remnants of it. Was he eating dinner when you got there?"

"I saw a lunchbox on his desk, but he hadn't started eating yet." She closed her eyes and smiled. "I don't know what was in that lunchbox, but it smelled just like my mother's chicken and dumplings with lots of garlic sauce. She's a fabulous cook."

Jax watched her. "Most mothers are. Was Sanders close with any of the performers?"

She broke away from her thoughts. "Honestly, he wasn't a very friendly sort, which is probably why none of the other employees attended his service. He was always strictly business with everyone. But tell me, Detective, why is it so significant that you didn't find his dinner that night? I toss the trash down the chute at the end of the hall in my building."

"His apartment doesn't have that convenience. Tenants are expected to empty their trash in the dumpster outside. And I couldn't find any sign of his metal lunch pail either."

"So, what does that mean?"

"I'm not sure yet." He looked at his notepad again. "How well do you know Robert Ashworth?"

She didn't like where this was going. "I think I'm done playing this game, Detective. Maybe your friend on the police force is right and you're making a mountain out of a molehill again. They don't think any crime has been committed. Besides, this is none of my business."

He smiled at her. "Oh, I think you're just as curious as I am to know what really happened. It's close to lunchtime. Can I buy you a hot dog? George usually sets his wagon up right around the corner."

"As I said, I have other commitments this afternoon."

"Our conversation stays between us, right?" he asked.

"Your secrets are safe with me, Detective." She said goodbye to Ace and got out of the car.

Jax watched her walk towards the front door of her apartment building. "Hey, Miss Graystone!" He saw her shoulders slump before she reluctantly turned around. "You never told me how you know so much about cars."

"And I think there's a whole lot more you're not telling me either, but as I said, it's none of my concern." She swung away from him, pulled the door open, and disappeared inside.

Jax sat there smiling. "She's an interesting woman, isn't she, Ace?" And very different than how he'd pegged her. Smarter, wittier, and even prettier than he first thought. She was very talented, too, and not just on stage. After everything that had just passed between them, he was more curious about how she knew how to fix a dirty throttle than anything else.

Although right now, he had a more pressing matter on his mind. His purpose for going to the cemetery wasn't to talk to Patricia Sanders. He wanted to find out who owned that new Rolls-Royce Silver Ghost that was parked down the street from her apartment yesterday. Then, he saw Robert Ashworth get into that same automobile.

7
A Case of Murder?

Jax pulled behind Tim's police car in front of the medical examiner's office. He saw Butch sitting in the passenger seat and prepared himself for one of Butch's smart remarks. But the man was fast asleep. Jax shook his head, made his way inside the building, and joined Tim and Doctor Norris in the other room.

"Doctor Norris was just telling me that he received Samuel Sanders' medical files this morning. He didn't have any known health issues," Tim told him. "He's ruling the cause of death as heart failure. Natural causes, Jax."

"It is quite common for heart problems to go undetected until it is too late," Doctor Norris stated.

Jax wasn't convinced. "I read a few articles about that green stuff around his mouth, Doctor, but I got lost in the jargon. Doesn't it have something to do with the gall bladder?"

"It is called bile, which is produced in the liver, travels through the gall bladder, and mixes with food to help digestion," Doctor Norris explained. "When a person becomes violently ill, and the contents of their stomach empties, bile can back up into the esophagus. Also, after a person dies, part of the decomposing process is the excretion of those purge fluids."

"A person's stomach needs to be empty to produce that bile?" Jax asked.

"That is correct. Judging from the sparse amount of vomit at the scene, I can only assume that Mister Sanders ate very little that day."

"So, he couldn't have consumed an entire meal of let's say, chicken and biscuits?"

"Jax..." Tim said.

"Hang on, Murph. I'm pretty sure he ate at least part of some sort of chicken dish before I found him."

"How do you know that?" Tim asked irritably.

"Well, if he did, he did not consume much," Doctor Norris said.

"Did you rule out botulism?" Jax asked, cutting to the quick. "If Sanders ate even a small amount of contaminated chicken, he'd get sick pretty quick on an empty stomach, wouldn't he? I like to think of myself as a gourmet cook, and I did a lot of reading about it since I didn't want to kill myself or Ace. When I was growing up, there was an outbreak of food poisoning from canned foods. Several kids at a local school got violently ill. Some were serious enough to end up in the hospital. I read that botulism can be deadly under certain circumstances and rapidly cause a whole slew of problems, like kidney and liver failure. Even paralysis. The way Sanders was sprawled out on his desk tells me that he was having difficulty with his motor control."

"We didn't find any food at the apartment, Jax," Tim reminded him.

"I know, Murph, and that's the problem. When Sanders got there, he was carrying his lunch pail, but it wasn't anywhere in the room when I found him. And it looked like someone had cleaned up pretty neatly after he died."

"Excuse me, gentlemen," Doctor Norris said. "I do not know anything about the man's lunchbox, but botulism and poisonous substances have become part of my routine analysis in circumstances such as this. Joe provided several samples of fluids, vomit residue, and such. I was able to isolate certain compounds in those samples and found them to consist of clean protein particles and plant-based substances, free of harmful chemicals and bacteria. In other words, healthy meat and vegetables."

"No disrespect, Doctor. I know you and the toxicologist have made terrific breakthroughs in detecting several deadly poisons. But aren't there others that still go undetected?" Judging from Doctor Norris' stern expression, Jax couldn't figure out whether he was contemplating the question or damning his insolence.

"Without any other evidence suggesting homicide, I stand by my conclusion, Detective," the Doctor stated firmly. "The man suffered from heart failure."

Tim snatched Jax's arm and pulled him towards the door. "Let's have a little talk outside. Thank you for your time, Doctor." As soon as they reached the sidewalk, Tim faced him. "Okay, Jax, I want to know right now. What did you take from the apartment the other night?"

"Not here with your deadbeat partner waiting for you," Jax told him. "It's close to noon. I will tell you everything after you drop Butch off at the station and meet me at L'Aiglon's."

"Where?"

"You know. That fancy restaurant on Fifty-Fifth Street."

"You're kidding me, right?"

"It won't take long, Murph, I promise."

"This better be good."

Jax headed south and parked his car near the restaurant. He filled Ace's water dish from the canteen sitting between the bucket seats. "I promise this is the last stop. If you need to do your business, go in the alley over there."

Inside the restaurant, the receptionist greeted him and summoned a waiter who led him into the dining room. As they made their way to the table in the corner, Jax noticed most of the patrons were dressed in their finest threads, with a few women wearing evening gowns and men in fancy black tuxedos. The ceilings were at least twenty feet high with a second-floor circular balcony overhead for additional tables. The room was elaborately decorated with hanging baskets of flowers, crystal chandeliers dangling from the gilded ceiling, and a large, fancy water fountain in the center.

When the young man pulled the chair out for him, he grabbed ahold of it. "Thanks. I've got it. I'll have a cup of java. I'm waiting for someone."

"My name is André and I will be your server today." He placed the menus on the table. "Our lunch specials consist of..."

"Just coffee for now. Is the manager around?"

"Our maître d' is otherwise engaged. May I be of service to you?"

"Who handles the meal deliveries to the Ambassador Theater?"

André hesitated. "Well, it is usually handled by Maître d' Blanchet. He is in the kitchen presently."

"Could you tell him that I'd like to speak with him for a minute?"

"Certainly, monsieur." And with a graceful pirouette, the young man twirled around and headed for the kitchen.

Jax felt someone's glare burning a hole through him. He glanced over at the next table, and an elderly woman sitting with her husband was staring back at him. He smiled. "How are you doing, ma'am?"

She quickly looked away and went back to her meal.

He leaned over to get a good look at their lunch plates, then picked up the menu. It was written in French, so he scanned through it. Then, André headed for his table carrying a cup in one hand and a silver pot in the other.

"The maître d' will join you as soon as he is available," he said as he poured the hot coffee for him. "As you can see, we have a busy lunch crowd."

"What kind of chicken dishes do you serve, André?"

"We have a delightful selection of *poitrine de poulet. Coq au vin* is a delicious chicken breast braised in our specialty aged red burgundy wine topped with champignons and lardons, which are nice, tasty mushrooms and cured bacon. We also have..."

"How about chicken and biscuits?"

André's grew irritated. "Of course, Monsieur. One of our regular lunch specials is *poulet à l'ail et biscuits*, a country-style dish with savory-sweet onions and tender slices of wild parsnips and carrots. Would you like me to order a platter for you?"

"Not yet. Thanks."

When the waiter left his table, he saw Tim walk into the restaurant. He stood up and flagged him down, ignoring the scowls he received from the other customers surrounding him.

Uncomfortably, Tim made his way through the dining room in full uniform and sat down. "What the heck are we doing here?"

Jax set the ceramic plate chip down in front of him. "I found that under Sanders' desk. He always ordered his dinner from this restaurant and had it delivered to the theater. Then, he would put it into his lunch pail and take it to his apartment. That night was no different. Before you ask, there was no way he could have disposed of the lunch pail, the rest of that plate, or anything else without me seeing him. The dumpster is on the side of the building in plain sight."

Tim picked up the chip to study it. "Jax, if you start flapping your gums about food poisoning, you're going to shut this place down. Then, there will be lawsuits, and all hell will break loose."

"Settle down, Murph. I don't think there was anything wrong with his meal when it was delivered. I think someone tampered with it afterward."

Tim leaned back in his seat. "Go on..."

"Whoever accepted the delivery at the theater put some kind of poison in his food, potent enough to kill him after a few bites. Then the killer waited until he was dead, went into his apartment, and cleaned up every trace of Sanders' meal. Except for that broken piece of plate. The landlord at the apartment took me down to the basement yesterday. There's a back door. He keeps it locked, but someone slipped in and out of the building without me seeing them. I'm sure of it."

Tim handed the chip back to him. "This could have been sitting under the desk for days or weeks."

"Yeah, so what happened to the containers his dinner was packed in, and his lunch pail? I'm telling you, Murph, this was murder. I shouldn't have waited so long before checking on Sanders that night, but I was only there to see if he was cheating on his wife. It never occurred to me that someone wanted him dead."

"His wife hired you?" Tim asked. "Was he cheating on her?"

"I don't think so."

"Did any women visit him at the apartment?"

"Well, one, but I'm pretty sure she only had a business relationship with him. I think it was just Patricia Sanders' wishful thinking since she needed solid grounds for divorce."

"Tell me about the woman you saw at the apartment," Tim said.

"Laura Graystone, but she went there to pick up a copy of a music script Sanders was writing, and she wasn't there long."

"Graystone. I've heard that name. How do you know that's why she went there?"

Jax chuckled thinking about it. "I interrogated her. Or maybe she interrogated me, I'm not sure which."

"For crying out loud, Jax, you can't go around questioning people and illegally searching other people's property. I don't understand why you're always dismissing police procedures and refusing to trust the experts. You said yourself that Doctor Norris was the best at what he does, and he determined that this wasn't murder. Why can't you just leave well enough alone?"

"You know why..." Jax said quietly.

Tim heaved a sigh. "That was two years ago, Jax. You've got to let the past go. You were instructed to follow police procedures or get fired. Everyone knows that incident wasn't your fault."

Jax swallowed hard and looked at him. "If I hadn't followed procedures, I could have saved that little boy's life. You and I both know that's why I quit the force."

"This situation is completely different."

"Is it? I was supposed to be watching Sanders that night, and he died right under my nose. It feels like the same situation to me."

A man dressed in a formal black suit approached them and his pencil-thin mustache widened with his grin. "Good day, Monsieurs. I am Maître d' Blanchet. André tells me that you are inquiring about our delivery services to the theaters?"

"The Ambassador is the only theater I'm interested in," Jax specified.

"How can I help you?"

"A friend of mine is performing there next Tuesday. She loves chicken and biscuits, and I wondered if I could have the meal delivered to her as a surprise around five o'clock."

"Ah, of course," he replied. "What a delightful gesture. We can certainly accommodate you. In fact, we have another patron who has a standing order for the same dish to be delivered to the Ambassador every Tuesday."

Not anymore, Jax wanted to tell him.

"I will let André serve you now. When you are finished with your lunch, I will return to gather the information from you."

"Excuse me," Jax said, stopping him. "Will it be delivered directly to her at the theater?"

"No, no. It is against the theater's policy. It will be given to the doorman, yet he understands our need for prompt service. Rest assured that your friend's meal will be piping hot and ready to eat when she receives it."

As soon as the man left, Jax tossed a few coins on the table to pay for his coffee and stood up. "C'mon, Murph. Time to go." And he led the way outside.

"What was all that about?" Tim asked.

"Do you know who Robert Ashworth is?"

"He owns the Ambassador Theater."

"Actually, his mother does." And Jax proceeded to tell him why he thought Robert Ashworth and Patricia Sanders were having an affair. "Whoever took Sanders' meal to him that day is my top suspect. I'm thinking Sanders' wife or Robert Ashworth, or both. She needed evidence of her husband's infidelity to file for divorce and be with Ashworth. Last Sunday, I told her that I hadn't come up with any proof yet. So, they resort to killing him.

She was at the theater right around the time his meal was delivered that day. I'd bet Ashworth was, too."

Tim started pacing back and forth across the sidewalk. "Jax, I can't tell my captain any of this gibberish. The Ashworths own most of the property in Manhattan. They're a powerful family and highly respected. Captain Ryan would fire me on the spot, especially since Doctor Norris determined Sanders died from a heart attack." He stopped, took a deep breath then turned to Jax. "All right, between you and me, let's say this wild theory of yours has some merit. Do you know who my top suspect would be? That Graystone woman since she was the last person to see Sanders alive."

8
Yankees vs. Boston Red Sox

Saturday, June 2

"Hurry up, girls! I don't want to miss the first inning!" Laura yelled as she waited for Jeanie and Margie by their front door. She wore her game-day uniform, knickers, a red and white middy sailor top, and her Red Sox ballcap. And she religiously carried her favorite leather baseball glove.

"Margie doesn't want to go," Jeanie told her, dressed far more formally in a casual mint-green drop-waist dress.

"Not go? But she promised she'd give baseball a chance. This is the third time she backed out on us, and it's the only Saturday I've had off in so long. Well, forget her, let's go." She swung the door open and hurried down the hall with Jeanie struggling to keep up.

They arrived at the new stadium in plenty of time for the first pitch. Laura bought their tickets, a bag of popcorn, and two sodas before settling into their seats between home plate and first base, several rows back. The Yankees were playing the Boston Red Sox, which has been Laura's favorite team since she grew up just west of Boston. She was only six-years-old when her father had taken her and her older brother to her very first ballgame against the New York Highlanders, the Yankees' original name. And they attended every game after that. Even after her father's death, she and her brother would attend the games as often as they could.

She loved the sport and their team. Of course, now that she was living in New York, it was difficult listening to the jeering crowd whenever the fans saw her colors, but she didn't care. Even though Babe Ruth, her favorite player, was traded to the Yankees three years ago, she was still a loyal Red Sox fan.

Jean, on the other hand, wasn't quite so enthusiastic about the sport. "I have a date tonight, Laura, so I can't stay for the whole game."

"You'll be home in plenty of time. It's only one o'clock. It'll be over by three. Now hush and stand up for the Star-Spangled Banner. The first game starts as soon as the band is finished." But as she proudly sang along with the crowd, Laura's focus was drawn away from the field to the opposite aisle seat, four rows down. "I don't believe this..."

"What's eating you, Laura?" Jeanie asked.

She remained silent until the tune was finished, and everyone started cheering. "That detective is here. The one I told you about."

"Where?"

Discreetly, she pointed. "Wouldn't you know it? There are twelve thousand people in the stadium, and he just happens to be sitting no more than an arm's length away from us."

"I can't see what he looks like," Jeanie said as she stood on tiptoes trying to get a better view.

"Well, at least he's not wearing that silly brown suit," Laura stated. And for a second, she thought he looked rather dapper in white pants and a sweater vest. But she quickly washed that traitorous thought out of her mind.

"He's sitting with another couple," Jeanie noticed. "Oh, look. That cute little girl just climbed into his lap. I wonder if that's his daughter?"

"I don't know, nor do I care." She plopped down in her seat and pulled the brim of her cap down over her brows.

She remained in that position, forcing herself to keep her

vision on the ballfield. Although every time Babe Ruth came to bat, she would move to the edge of her seat knowing the damage that he could do. By the fifth inning, she slumped in her seat watching Boston fall behind three runs while the massive crowd was still on their feet, whistling, clapping, and cheering.

During the next two innings, Laura forgot all about Jax and kept her eyes peeled on the game. With a sudden burst of energy, Boston retaliated with two runs in the top of the sixth, and a whopping four runs in the seventh. She was so engrossed in the game, she didn't realize the seventh inning stretch had just been called, and Jax was heading up the stairs towards her.

"Miss Graystone, what a surprise," he stated, standing beside her.

Slowly, she looked up at him. "Hello, Detective Diamond."

"I didn't peg you for a baseball fan. Of course, judging from your ballcap you're rooting for the wrong team."

Jeanie leaned forward. "Hello. I'm Jeanie. Laura's best friend."

"Nice to meet you, Jeanie."

"Likewise," she replied, smiling.

"I'm heading for the concession stand. Would either of you ladies like a bag of popcorn or a soda?"

"Not me. I've got to fly," Jeanie said as she got to her feet. "This isn't as much fun as I thought it would be, Laura. I feel bad ditching you like this, but Bobby is picking me up at five o'clock, and I have no idea what I'm going to wear." She looked up at Jax. "Would you mind keeping Laura company for the rest of the game, Detective? You'd be doing me a huge favor."

Laura stood up. "Jeanie!"

"I'm sorry, Laura. I'll catch a trolley home." She squeezed around Laura, said goodbye to them, and hurried off.

Laura sat down in a huff.

"C'mon, Miss Graystone. It'll be fun watching the rest of the game together being on opposite sides and all."

"That isn't necessary, Detective. I've watched plenty of ball games by myself. Apparently, I don't choose my friends very well."

"Nonsense, I won't hear of it. And call me Jax."

She eyed him. "Is that your real name? Or is it Jack or John?"

"Just Jax. I come from a big family, and I guess my parents had a sense of humor. They sure did love playing card games. I've got to get a couple of sodas for my friends. Do you want to join me?"

The crowd started singing, *Take Me Out to the Ballgame*, so she shook her head and started singing along just to be rid of him. He finally left and for a while, she considered moving to another seat or leaving the stadium altogether before he returned. The last thing she wanted to do was socialize with Detective Diamond, and she was furious with Jeanie for leaving her high and dry like this.

But she peered over her shoulder, deep in thought.

She might not be in the mood to play quid pro quo with him again, but she did have a few more questions. Despite what she'd said yesterday, she was curious to know if there was something more to Mister Sanders' death, especially after his wife's reaction to her at the funeral. So, she sat there undecided until it was too late to make her getaway.

Jax passed out the drinks to his friends, then approached her and handed her a bottle of Coca-Cola. "What did I miss?"

She moved over into Jean's seat. "Your team is still behind, three to six. Who are your friends?"

"That's Tim, his wife, and their two little ones, Lizzie and Petey. Tim's the police sergeant I told you about."

"The one who said you always make a mountain out of a mole hill?"

He laughed. "Yeah."

"So, you're from a big family?" she asked off-handedly, simply for a bit of chit-chat before she got to the point of this.

"There were twelve of us, I think. I fell somewhere in the middle. Not the youngest, not the oldest. It was the safest place to be."

She kept her eyes on the ballfield. "Where are you from?"

"I'm an apple knocker from upstate New York."

"Really? I would have pegged you for a city boy."

"Nope. Country-bred for sure. Cows, horses, fresh air, and green fields as far as you can see."

She looked over at him. Why didn't she believe him?

"What about you?" he asked. "Do you have any brothers or sisters?"

"I'm surprised you don't have your notepad with you to jot down my answer."

He laughed. "I'm not working today."

"I have an older brother," she told him.

"Is he the one who taught you how to fix a dirty throttle?"

A laugh escaped her. "You're dying to know, aren't you? My father used to race cars and had his own repair shop. My brother and I kept it going after he died."

"I'm sorry. About your father, I mean."

"He's been gone twelve years. I've had plenty of time to accept it."

"Losing a parent is tough no matter how much time has passed."

His response surprised her. "Detective? How did you know about my meetings with Mister Sanders?" When he didn't reply right away, she admitted, "I think his wife knew about them. At the funeral, she didn't seem very pleased when I told her who I was."

"She doesn't know about them," he assured her. "She suspected her husband was seeing someone else, but she only guessed it might be you."

Laura stared down at the ballfield again, feeling bad about it anyway. "It wasn't anything like that."

"Do you mind if I ask you a question? What happens to a new manuscript after the playwright finishes it? You said Sam Sanders gave you a copy, and he was working on the original. Who would he give the final copy to?"

She broke away from her thoughts. "The theater director usually. He decides whether it's worth the investment or not.

Then it needs to be approved by the theater owner, I think. What did the police do with Mister Sanders' original script?"

"I couldn't find it at the apartment. Do you know if he gave a copy to anyone else?"

"Mister Beacham, our piano player has one. He said he was going to give his copy to Director Rosenberg."

She wanted to ask him why he was so interested in the manuscript, but they noticed the ballgame was over, and everyone was leaving their seats. "Did we win the game?"

"Yeah, seven to three. Go ahead and gloat all you want."

She stood up to leave. "I wouldn't dream of rubbing your nose in it."

He motioned for her to leave first. "Can I give you a ride home?"

She hesitated. This was all very strange. At the theater, she didn't like him right off and had wanted to avoid him at all costs. And what were the chances that she'd run into him here at ballgame of all places? Yet, he didn't seem like such a bad fella. "I suppose so."

Tim and his family were following the crowd up the steps. Jax shouted to them, waved goodbye to the kids, and he and Laura left the stadium. He escorted her to his car that was parked on River Avenue and opened the door for her.

She glanced up to thank him and with the sunlight shining down, she was struck by the brilliant color of his eyes again. "Are you as smart as I think you are?"

He couldn't keep a straight face. "If I was so smart, I wouldn't be working as a private detective, would I?"

"Well, I can think of worse careers. You know, I am rather hungry. Can I take you up on your offer for one of those hot dogs now?"

"You're reading my mind, but I need to stop at my place for a minute if that's okay. I want to check on Ace. I hate leaving him alone for too long."

"Where do you live?"

He smiled at her. "Right around the corner from you on Carlton Avenue."

"Well, isn't that a coincidence?"

"Yeah, I thought so, too," he chuckled. But as they traveled down the street, he quickly lost his smile and furiously started pumping the brake pedal. "Hang on, Laura. Something's wrong with the brakes."

She groaned. "I told you to take Old Nellie to a mechanic." But she sat upright nervously when he yanked the steering wheel to the left to avoid smashing into the car in front of them.

The car jerked into the opposite lane and thankfully, the oncoming traffic quickly moved out of their way. Yet, drivers were screaming and cursing, and honking their horns.

"Yeah, same to you, Mister!" Jax shouted back. He clutched the steering wheel so tightly his knuckles went white as they swerved in and out of both lanes, trying not to hit anyone on the street crammed full of cars, bicyclists, and pedestrians.

"Use the brake lever!" Laura yelled above the clatter, but he was too busy trying to avoid a collision. And they both panicked when they saw the trolley pulling out in front of them heading east, across both lanes. "Quick, Jax. Turn down that side road! Stop pumping the pedal if it's not working. Just get off this road and don't hit anything. I'll work on the lever."

Laura grabbed the brake lever while he made the turn, but even though the side road was free of other cars, it inclined down a steep hill, and the car picked up speed. Laura discovered the lever was stuck, and she tried to remain as calm as possible while shoving it forward and pulling it back without breaking it off.

Up ahead, they saw a group of teenagers playing catch in the middle of the road. Jax yelled for them to get out of the way, then he swore under his breath. With all his might, he yanked the steering wheel to the left again, and they headed straight for the butcher shop on the corner.

Seconds before the car crashed into the building, they lurched to a sudden stop, throwing Jax against the steering wheel, and Laura fell into the dashboard. When they glanced up, the car was sitting only six feet away from the wooden structure.

Jax took a deep breath while Laura caught hers.

"Thank goodness the lever brake finally kicked in," she said quietly.

But they heard a grinding noise. "Get out of the car, Laura!" They both jumped out and stood there while the car slowly rolled forward, smack into the three-foot brick wall around the base of the shop. "Are you all right?"

"I am now," she told him. "And you?"

"I'm just glad you were with me. I guess you're right. It's time to take Old Nellie to the repair shop."

She rolled her eyes. "While you talk to the shop owner who looks angry enough to start a fight with you, I'm going to take a look under the hood."

9
Elements of a Murderer

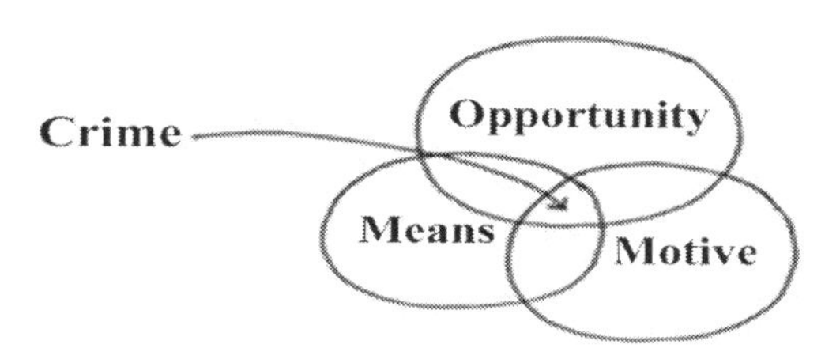

Jax led the way to his apartment on the first floor. "Good thing those teenagers were there to help us push my car into the alley. And it was nice of Tony to give us a lift home."

"I don't know how you managed to make friends with him," Laura grumbled. "We nearly destroyed his shop."

"Tony was great. He even gave us a couple of free pounds of lamb chops." Jax opened the door and motioned to her. "Ladies first."

Ace greeted them both, and he was especially happy to see Laura. She squatted down to pet him while Jax tossed the chops on the kitchen counter. He grabbed two bottles of beer from the icebox and poured one into a glass for Laura. She joined him in the kitchen, and he handed it to her.

"We both could use something to calm us down," he told her.

"Isn't liquor against the law?"

"Only if you're caught. Drink up. That was a bit of a scare."

She wasn't about to argue with him and gladly took a few sips.

"Since I'm stuck without a car, how about I make us dinner? I can fry up a couple of those lamb chops, and I have plenty of mashed potatoes and buttered green beans to go with it."

She stared at him, curiously. "You don't know anything

about cars, but you can cook?"

"Yeah, funny, huh?"

"I spent more time in my father's repair shop than in the kitchen. I do miss my mother's homemade meals."

"Then you're in for a treat. Make yourself at home. It won't take long."

"Does Ace need to go outside?" she wondered.

"He's fine. I rigged up a rubber flap on the back door so he can come and go as he pleases."

Curiously, she wandered into the living room to see it for herself, but she was distracted as she glanced around. The small room was simply furnished with a beige sofa, a wing-back chair, an oak coffee table, and a matching bookcase. Everything was noticeably clean and tidy, in complete contrast to his disheveled appearance at the theater.

She saw the bookcase was full and pulled out a couple of books to flip through them. They all appeared to be crime-related, both fictional and non-fiction. Then, she noticed the lone photograph sitting on top of the case. It was a group portrait of the thirteenth police precinct, according to the sign in the photo. And in the back row, she recognized Jax.

"You were on the police force?" she called to him.

He peeked into the room. "Oh, the photo. Yeah, for a couple of years, but I prefer working on my own."

She joined him in the kitchen again and leaned against the doorjamb while Ace laid down beside her. "I imagine you've made a few enemies working on the force and as a detective."

"None that I know of. I get along with everyone."

She waited a moment. "Well, someone tampered with your car."

He stopped cooking to look at her.

"From what I could see, the bands around your front brake drums looked like they had been partially cut rather than frayed from wear and tear."

He turned to flip the lamb chops in the frying pan and stir the beans. "Maybe I do have an enemy or two out there."

"It smells delicious. Can I at least set the table?"

"Sure. The plates are in the bottom cupboard of the Hoosier cabinet."

She grabbed two plates and pulled open the drawer, looking for silverware.

"We need three plates," he told her.

"Three?"

He pointed to Ace.

She smiled and snatched another plate.

When Jax finished cooking, he cut the meat off the bones for Ace. Then he slathered the lamb and potatoes with gravy, piled the beans high on each plate, and served them.

Laura stared at it. "I'm speechless. This looks and smells amazing."

"Hopefully, it's as good as it looks. Why don't you tell me more about yourself? Where are you from?"

Briefly, Laura told him that she grew up in Millbury, Massachusetts, and her parents owned a home on Blackstone River. She explained that her mother was a music teacher at the local high school, which is how she became interested in singing and dancing. Then, she finished with how she ended up in the Follies here in the city.

"Without Missus Ashworth, I would still be performing at the small playhouse in Whalom." She stopped eating, but only for a second. "Honestly, these are the best lamb chops and gravy I've ever had. But don't ever tell my mother I said that."

"Did the Ashworths help you get the lead in your current play?" he asked. "From what I hear, you've got plenty of talent, but nailing the lead in a Broadway play so soon after you arrived in the city couldn't have been easy."

"I'm sure Missus Ashworth pulled some strings. The theater also needed to fill the part as quickly as possible after the death of the original leading actress."

"What happened to her?"

"You must have read about Kitty Cooper in the newspapers last March. Someone broke into her apartment and killed her."

"I heard about it. Did you know her?"

"No, we never met. Annie, my assistant, worked for her and didn't like her very much. Although, I don't think Annie likes anyone. You met her when you came to the theater."

"She seems to be very fond of you."

"I don't know why. For some reason, we just hit it off." Laura set her fork down. "It was kind of eerie taking Kitty Cooper's place in the musical, especially under those circumstances." She'd nearly cleaned her plate and pushed it away. "Dinner was delicious. Thank you."

"Did you want another helping?"

"No, I couldn't eat another bite. Jax, you think Mister Sanders was murdered, don't you?"

"I can't prove it yet, but there was some sort of poison in his food or drink. And whoever put it there cleared away every trace of his dinner afterward."

"And you think they took his new manuscript, too? Is that why you were asking so many questions about it at the ball-game?"

"It disappeared, so it has some importance."

She picked up Ace's empty plate, and her own, and carried them to the sink.

"How about I get us another beer, and we can sit in the living room?" he suggested. "I'll take care of the dishes later."

"The least I can do is help clean up." She turned the water on while he gathered the pots and pans, scraped leftovers into the trash basket, and placed the utensils in the sink. "No wonder you asked me so many questions at the theater," she whispered. "If it was murder, then it's natural to think that I had something to do with it since I was the last person to see Mister Sanders."

Jax shut the water off. He turned her towards him and looked at her directly. "Laura, there are three important aspects needed to find and convict a criminal, motive, means, and opportunity. Maybe you had the opportunity by being at Sanders' apartment that night, but you certainly didn't have a motive. Not when he wrote a play that would have advanced your career.

And I guarantee, you didn't have the means. It takes a lot of planning and premeditation to poison someone. Basically, a pretty rotten person."

She lowered her head, nodding slowly.

"Look, we've both had enough excitement for one day. Why don't I walk you home?"

"It's just a couple of blocks. I can manage on my own."

"Nonsense. Ace needs the exercise anyway. C'mon."

They walked down the street together with Ace in front of them, leading the way. Jax carried most of the conversation now, telling her a few funny stories about his family to lighten her mood. He talked about his brief stint in the army, but since their military didn't enter the war until it was nearly over, he never traveled overseas. And he shared how he had found Ace abandoned in an alley a little over a year ago when he was a puppy.

"We've been together ever since. He's as smart and loyal as they come."

"And beautiful, too. But look. He just sat down in front of my apartment building. How does he know where I live?"

"We dropped you off here yesterday after the funeral, remember?"

"I guess he *is* smart. Thank you, Jax. It was...well, an interesting day to say the least."

"Are you busy tomorrow? It's Sunday and Ace and I usually spend a few hours in the park. I promise it won't be as exciting as today."

She laughed. "What time?"

"We'll come by for you about ten if that's okay." She agreed, and he watched her until she was safely inside the building, then he headed home. "You like her, don't you, Ace?" Jax glanced back at her apartment building. "Yeah, me, too."

As soon as he got home, he called Tim. He knew his friend would throw a fit when he found out that Laura was the woman he was with at the ballgame. So, he ignored the lecture, cut Tim off, and told him what had happened to his car. After he mentioned the brakes were deliberately cut, he told Tim that Laura knew plenty about automobiles, and credited her for stopping the car in the nick of time.

Then, he asked Tim to pull the Kitty Cooper files at the station so he could have a look at them. When that request went about as well as the rest of their conversation, he said goodbye and hung up the phone.

Jax finished cleaning up the kitchen and grabbed another beer. He sat on the sofa with Ace, trying to fit all the pieces together with what he knew. One thing is for sure. Kitty Cooper's and Sam Sanders' deaths had more in common than just the lilies that were planted at the murder scenes. Laura had a connection to both victims. She had replaced Kitty in the current play, and Sam had written a new play for her. He wasn't sure how it was all related, but again, he wondered who had tampered with his car brakes? And why?

At eight o'clock the next morning, Jax woke up abruptly. He'd fallen asleep on the sofa, and it took him a minute to gather his bearings. But someone was furiously pounding on his door. "I'm coming!" he yelled, and he finally swung the door open.

Tim charged inside, slapping a manila folder against his chest. "What are you cooking for breakfast? I'm hungry."

Jax saw Kitty Cooper's name written on the front of the folder and smiled. "I'll make us eggs and bacon."

"And lots of coffee." Tim went into the kitchen with Jax following along. "Gus isn't happy with me for waking him up so early this morning. He said he checked your car out yesterday and agreed that someone had cut the brake cables. You made somebody pretty mad besides me, Jax."

He heated a pot of water and pulled out a carton of eggs and a slab of bacon. "Didn't Kitty Cooper die after inhaling too much chloroform?"

"Some cornballs use it socially to replace alcohol, which is why we determined her death was a suicide at first."

"Yeah, but after Doctor Norris performed the autopsy, he was sure it was murder, and chloroform had been used as the weapon, right?"

"That's how she died, but we couldn't prove who was responsible. Our best guess is a couple of hoodlums broke into her apartment, and it was a robbery that went too far. Now, tell me about your new girlfriend."

Jax laughed. "You'll meet her later. At least I hope you will. We're taking Ace to the park this morning, and I thought I'd invite her to your place for dinner. It's Sunday, and Carla usually makes spaghetti. Laura loves homecooked meals."

"This is all fun and games to you, isn't it, Jax? For crying out loud, it is not a joke. Gus said that you could have been killed if your car had smashed into the butcher shop at full speed."

"Luckily, my *new girlfriend* knows more about cars than I do." He poured them both a cup of coffee and sat down. "Remember my wild theory about Patricia Sanders and Robert Ashworth conspiring to murder her husband? Even though Laura knows a lot about cars, I'm sure Patricia Sanders is clueless. She or Ashworth could have hired someone to cut the brake cables on my car."

"To stop you from looking deeper into it?"

"Of course, that just makes me want to dig deeper."

Tim gulped down the rest of his coffee. "Cripes. Now, you've got *me* believing your dang theory. And you're sure your girlfriend isn't part of it?"

"Nope. You'll see why later when you meet her."

"Well, be careful, Jax. And I hope for your sake she's not playing you."

10

Coney Island

Sunday, June 3

Laura peeked out the window in her bedroom and saw Ace sitting in front of her building with Jax standing beside him. She smiled, quickly looked at herself in the mirror again, and made her way downstairs. Ace saw her come out the front door and ran over to greet her. Jax followed along, and she gladly wrapped her arm in his when he offered.

It was a beautiful day with cloudless skies, bright sunshine, and the perfect temperature. As they strolled along toward Fort Greene Park, less than a half-mile away, they talked about absolutely nothing of importance. Laura was glad since the latter part of yesterday had turned out to be a bit too intense. Although already it seemed that no matter what went on, Jax remained fairly calm, even saying something humorous to ease the tension.

"There's a lot of history here," he told her when they reached the park. "During the Revolutionary War, the military built several forts here and named the park after Nathaniel Greene, a heroic general in the Continental Army. The monument was built about the same time to honor the thousands of prisoners who died aboard British ships during the war."

"I've noticed the tower when I pass by the park, but I never knew what it represented. I'm ashamed to say that haven't had the opportunity to explore much of the city the past few months."

"You haven't? Well, that settles it. We're going exploring today. There are so many terrific things to see and do here. And I promise not to bore you with a lot of tour guide jargon. We'll start with a few of my favorite pastimes."

And that began a day of sightseeing for them. They played catch with Ace in the park for a while. Then, they strolled along the walkway around the pond that was encompassed by a dense forest of beautiful flowering shrubs and bushes. The water glistened in the sunlight, colorful dragon flies fluttered by them, and frogs merrily hopped around the lily pads. It was a heavenly paradise tucked within a vast and busy city.

Afterward, they walked to the bay to ride the ferry around the Statue of Liberty. Jax stopped at the ticket booth and reached into his pocket for a few coins. A penny dropped to the ground, and just as he bent down to pick it up, Laura kicked it out of his reach.

"Leave it be," she told him. "It landed tails-up."

"Huh?"

"Trust me, Jax. We don't need any more bad luck. If it had landed heads-up, you'd be good to go."

"Tails-up is bad luck, and heads-up is good luck?"

"Yes. I know it's annoying, but everyone has some annoying traits. Even you."

"Well, I can't think of one offhand, but I'm sure you're right."

They boarded the ferry, and as it traveled across the waters, Jax explained the significance of both the statue and Ellis Island not far away. Laura listened intently while enjoying her first ferry ride. Yet, she kept her gaze fixed upon the magnificent lady of peace, as Jax referred to her. The enormous copper sculpture was as rich in history as it was breath-taking, and the mere sight of her was mesmerizing. Even Ace seemed to enjoy the ride as much as she did. He sat beside them with his head poked through the railing, reveling in the breeze.

From there, they snuck Ace on a trolley and headed for the amusement parks at Coney Island where they spent the rest of the afternoon. Jax told her that this was Ace's favorite place of all. He loved the crowds, especially the children who always shared their snacks with him.

Laura was stunned by the swarms of people, the endless street hawkers selling an array of different foods, the wide variety of rides, and the deafening yet joyous sounds of laughter, singing, bells, and whistles.

"Back home, we had a few local festivals during the summer, and the traveling carnival passed through town once in a great while," she said. "I've never seen anything like this before."

Jax grabbed her hand. "We'll start you out slow and work our way up."

They went on the carousel and Ferris wheel, and they took a ride on the miniature train. Next, they attempted to walk through the rolling barrel with both of them falling several times and laughing so hard. Ace smartly remained on the sidelines, watching them and barking every time they fell.

Next, they went on the Teaser, which were swings that circled high in the air, and the Tickler, where they sat in spinning wooden chairs. Then, Jax took her on the small bumping cars that dipped and rolled over waves of steel. But when they approached the Steeplechase Course, Laura stopped dead in her tracks and refused to go any further.

The ride was set up similar to a racetrack for horses that circled around a quarter-mile track. Eight mechanical horses were propped on steel poles, like those on the carousel, and when the bell rang, they moved forward around the hilly track to begin the race.

"You are not getting me on that!" she yelled over the laughter around them.

"C'mon, Miss Graystone," Jax ribbed. "I was just starting to think you were an adventurous woman."

"I'm sticking with Ace on this one. He's smarter than both of us."

"Suit yourself. I guess I'll have to win the race all by myself." He winked at her, paid for the ride, and he chose his horse.

Before the ride even began, Laura practically doubled over with laughter seeing him sitting atop one of the horses, smiling over at her. The bell finally rang, and the horses moved forward rather rapidly, surprising Jax, so he clung tighter.

Laura watched Jax's horse go around the course, but Ace started growling, then barking, and he suddenly ran off. She twirled around to see where he went. She kept shouting to him, but her voice was lost within the commotion around her. She couldn't see him anywhere within the crowd. She didn't know what to do, whether to go after him or not. Yet, within a few minutes, he made his way back to her.

She bent down to pet him, and he licked her cheek. "Are you okay, Ace?"

The ride had ended, and Jax hurried over to them. "I saw Ace run off. Is everything okay? Was anyone bothering you, Laura?"

"No, he just started barking and took off through the crowd."

"He saw something he didn't like," Jax said as he scanned the area. "Let's get something to eat. Maybe he's hungry."

Later, after they'd had their fill of hot dogs and treats, and a few more rides, they wandered towards the section of games to play for a nickel. Jax caught Laura's arm and held her back. "You like watching baseball. Can you throw one?"

She glanced over at the milk bottle pyramid and shrugged her shoulders. So, he led her over to the game and set two nickels down. The man behind the counter took the coins and handed each of them three baseballs.

"As always, ladies first," Jax said.

She picked up one of the balls. Then, she glanced up at Jax and winked at him. The gesture confused him until she threw the ball overhand and hit the pyramid dead center, knocking all the bottles over. She held in a chuckle. "Must have been beginners' luck." But her next two balls were thrown just as accurately, and the man handed her a cute little rubber duck for a prize.

"I'm not even going to try and top that," Jax told her, and he pushed his three baseballs over to her. After she knocked over each one of those bottles, she traded her duck for a small stuffed rabbit. Jax took her hand and led her away. "I guess we need to find a more challenging game for you."

They played the Ring Toss game, Balloon Darts, and the Fishbowl game. Laura won each of them, beating Jax, and he trailed behind her, carrying one of two small stuffed rabbits, a two-foot lion, and a goldfish swimming in a mason jar filled with water. As they continued walking, Jax saw the Kissing Booth was next. He flashed Laura a hopeful grin, but she laughed and shook her head.

Then, his eyes lit up. "Well, we're coming up to the shooting gallery. I know I can give you a run for your money on this game."

The man set them up with their own pellet rifles. He told them that to win a prize, they had five shots, and they needed to hit all five plastic, yellow ducks moving in a line across the backboard. Smugly, Jax insisted upon going first this time, so Laura stood back and watched him.

He picked up the rifle and skillfully nestled it against his shoulder. Ever so carefully, he kept his eyes on the ducks and pulled the trigger. One by one, he hit five ducks and won a little pink rubber lamb. And he stood there proudly holding his prize.

Laura burst out laughing. She picked up the rifle, still giggling, and without really trying, she quickly took her shots. And she hit a duck every time.

Jax couldn't believe it. "Are you pulling my leg? I thought you said there weren't many carnivals where you come from."

She laughed even harder. "There aren't! But I had an older brother. He taught me how to play baseball, and we used to go skeet shooting all the time."

"Yeah, well I grew up with seven brothers, and this is embarrassing." But Jax caught sight of the next game, and his irritation fled. "Now there's a game I know I can win." He picked up her stuffed animals and the goldfish, called to Ace who seemed glued to Laura's side, and marched over to the *Strongman* game.

Jax handed the man a coin and picked up the mallet. He tipped his head up to look at the bell, his target which was seventeen feet high. Then, he easily slammed the mallet down on the platform, and the bell rang. Determined to win Laura the largest stuffed animal they had, he played the game six more times and hit the bell each time. Proudly, he handed her the three-foot teddy bear.

"Well done, Detective Diamond," she smirked.

"Yeah, it's about time, too." But he checked his wristwatch and noticed it was going on seven o'clock. "Murph is going to be plenty mad at me now. I told him that we'd be at his place for dinner by five."

"That was a little presumptuous of you, wasn't it?"

"I figured we'd have such a fun time, you couldn't refuse. Besides, Carla makes the best spaghetti and meatballs around, although we missed dinner by now."

"I couldn't possibly eat anything else, anyway," she said, squeezing her big stuffed bear. "I think we went through four or five Coney dogs, not to mention the cotton candy, funnel cakes, and root beer floats."

"So, is it okay if we stop by on our way home? We can go on a few more rides first if you want."

"I've had my fill of those, too, and I'd like to meet your friends."

He quickly collected all of her winnings, and they headed down the boardwalk. The beach was swarming with people, and the bay glistened in the sunlight just beyond them. The scene and being near the water again reminded her of her parents' home by the river, and she inhaled a deep breath of air.

"It was a fabulous day, Jax. I had so much fun."

"I'm glad. I did, too."

After they took the trolley back to Fulton Street, they headed down the sidewalk. Jax told her that Tim only lived about four blocks down, and as they passed several shops, Laura wondered what in the world she was going to do with goldfish and all the stuffed animals. Jax suggested that she give them to Tim's children, and she thought it was a great idea.

But she suddenly stopped walking. She grabbed Jax's shirt sleeve and dragged him closer to the brick building beside them.

"What is it?" he asked worriedly.

"There's an outdoor cafe up ahead," she whispered.

He glanced over. "What about it?"

"Robert Ashworth is at one of the tables. I think he's there with Missus Sanders."

Jax leaned over to get a better look and saw the two of them together. "Yeah, it's them all right. Let's not interrupt their little *tête-à-tête*. We'll backtrack and take the long way around." He motioned for them to head down the street behind them.

She led the way, but once they turned the corner, she stood there glaring at him. "I'm shocked to see those two together, and at a cheap little cafe on Fulton Street of all places. But you didn't act surprised at all."

"When I mentioned Robert Ashworth to you the other day, you got mad at me and ended our conversation. So, I figured you wouldn't want to hear what I know about him."

"Well, I do now!"

He laughed. "Okay, I'll tell you about it on our way to Murph's' place."

They started walking again, but she kept glaring at him. "Can you speak French?"

"A little. My mother was born in France."

"And yet, you had such a difficult time saying 'L'Aiglon's Restaurant' when you questioned me at the theater."

"I just wanted to see if you could say it," he chuckled.

"You can be so childish sometimes."

"Yeah, but that's what makes me so much fun."

11
Broadway Butterfly

Tim swung the door open and scowled at Jax. "You're late."

"I know, Murph. We lost track of time. I'd like you to meet Laura Graystone. Laura, this is my best friend and partner, Tim Murphy."

"Ex-partner," Tim corrected.

"Nice to meet you," Laura greeted.

Tim nodded to her yet kept his glower on Jax while Ace raced past him into the apartment.

"Laura has never been to Coney Island, so we spent the day there," Jax explained, and they both brushed by him. "Sorry we missed dinner."

"You didn't miss it," Tim snapped. "Carla refused to let us eat until you got here."

Laura's eyes grew horrified, and Jax burst out laughing. "I think we've had our fill of food for one day."

"Well, I think you're both going to get your fill of Carla's spaghetti. Ace, too."

"Okay, okay," Jax chuckled. "Help us with these toys, will you?" He shoved them in Tim's arms, and yelled, "Lizzie! Petey! We have surprises for you!" And the kids came running.

Jax introduced Laura to Carla and the kids, and they all sat at the dinner table together. Laura watched Jax clean his plate while she struggled to eat as much as she could just to be polite. And on the floor beside her, even Ace had a tough time finishing his meal. But the conversation flowed, with Carla carrying the bulk of it. She mentioned that she and her friends had heard about the new starlet on Broadway, and she was thrilled to meet Laura. She asked her a thousand questions about her career, and the different performers she knew.

Laura helped clear off the table afterward and followed Carla into the kitchen. When they had finished washing the dishes, they joined the others in the living room. Jax was sitting in the wing-back chair with both Lizzy and Petey on his lap and seeing them together warmed her heart.

"Time for bed, little ones!" Carla announced. Lizzy and Petey hugged and kissed Jax goodnight, then they did the same with Laura, and thanked her for all the new toys. Carla carried all the stuffed animals while Ace led the way down the hall to their bedroom.

Laura sat on the couch. "Your children are adorable, Tim. And Carla is very nice. Thank you for dinner. It's been an exciting day all around."

"You're welcome, Laura," Tim said. "I heard you and Jax had a bit of excitement yesterday, too."

Jax scowled at him. "When they were in the kitchen, I told you not to get into any of that tonight?"

"It's okay," Laura said. "Are you going to look into who might have cut those brake cables?"

Tim nodded. "It was probably the same person who was following you around at the park today."

Jax groaned. "Can't you keep anything between us, Murph?"

She sat upright. "Someone was following us?"

"It was probably just my imagination. And Ace's," Jax added under his breath. Then he quickly changed the subject. "Laura is quite the little hustler at those carnival games."

"Tim, did Jax tell you that we saw Robert Ashworth and

Patricia Sanders together on our way over here?" she asked. "Do you think they had something to do with Mister Sanders' death?"

Jax leaned forward in his chair, watching her. "Laura, let's not get into..."

"I'm still not convinced it *was* murder," Tim replied, ignoring him. "The medical examiner said it was heart failure, and there's no substantial proof stating otherwise. On top of that, now Jax is trying to connect Kitty Cooper's murder with Sanders' death. It's ridiculous."

Jax held his hand over his eyes. "I didn't tell her about that either, Murph."

"Kitty Cooper?" Laura asked. "Jax and I were talking about her last night."

"She was a Broadway butterfly," Tim said. "Like butterflies, some women come to the theater district attracted by all the flashy lights, and fame. Then, they get all caught up with wealthy bootleggers and gangsters."

"What could her death possibly have to do with Mister Sanders'?"

"The woman had a white lily in her hair when we found her body," Jax explained indignantly as he glared at Tim. "Sanders had the same type of flower pinned to his jacket. So yes, I do believe the cases are related. And I think Robert Ashworth and Patricia Sanders killed them both. I just need to find something tying the two of them to Kitty Cooper."

Laura stood up and wandered over to the window with her mind reeling.

"See, Murph," Jax spouted. "You upset her. I told you not to bring any of this up tonight."

Slowly, she turned towards them. "My friend, Jeanie, told me the other day that she'd heard a rumor Robert Ashworth had an affair with Kitty Cooper."

"Robert and Kitty?" Jax stood up. "Tim, Lieutenant Simmons questioned Robert Ashworth after Kitty's death, but according to those files you gave me, it was only about Kitty's work schedule that day. Were you with the Lieutenant when he questioned Ashworth?"

"No. And I never heard any rumors."

"Why would you?" Jax asked. "You're not part of the theater crowd. Well, that just opened up..."

"Pandora's box!" Tim squawked as he jumped to his feet. "You're both trying to tie more knots into the rope when they all just keep falling apart."

Carla joined them again with Ace. "Keep your voice down, Tim. The kids are nearly asleep."

Jax went over and took Laura's hand. "Thanks for dinner, Carla. We've had a long day and I should get Laura back home."

"You're leaving?" she asked.

"We'll do it again soon. I promise." He kissed Carla's cheek, and Laura thanked them both before they headed out the door.

"That wasn't very nice, Jax," Laura said as they made their way downstairs. "I feel bad leaving so quickly."

"When Murph gets all tied up in knots, he just keeps going on and on. He needs some time to calm down and sleep on it." He held the front door open for her. "Besides, I know Carla. If we had stayed a minute longer, she would have forced us to eat about half a dozen of her cannoli."

"Oh. They are both very sweet, though. Carla made me feel right at home. And it's easy to see that Lizzy and Petey simply adore you and Ace."

He squeezed her hand. "How about you?"

She laughed. "I adore Ace. I'm still undecided about you."

"Yeah, I kind of grow on people I guess, so give it a little more time."

"Jax, will you tell me now why you thought someone was following us at the amusement park?"

"Not tonight, Laura. I'm walking down the street with a beautiful woman, the moon is shining, and the sky is filled with stars. It doesn't get any more romantic than this."

His sentiment silenced her. He was a curious fella, for sure. A bundle of contradictions. He had transformed from his wrinkled brown suit to the stylish crème-colored sweater and pants he was wearing now. He could be both exasperating and humorous, boldly honest and secretive, and while he was tall and slender, the fact that he had so easily rung the bell at the Strongman game six times in a row proved that he was stronger than he appeared. And with it all, he was a perfect gentleman.

When they reached her apartment building, Jax and Ace walked her to the door. "When do you go back to work?" he asked.

"I have a rehearsal at the theater tomorrow, but our next performance isn't until Wednesday night. I'm looking forward to getting back into the routine."

He opened the door for her. "Can I call you this week?"

"I'd like that," she told him, and she turned to leave.

"Hold on. Take this." He handed her a small card with his telephone number on it. "You can call me, too. Just in case you miss me." He winked at her and left with Ace.

But Laura lost her smile. She looked at the card, then at him again, wondering why the tone of voice had sounded more worried than playful.

Monday, June 4

"Did he kiss you goodnight?" Jeanie asked excitedly when Laura met her and Margie in their apartment for coffee the next morning.

"No, of course not! I barely know him."

"He made you dinner on Saturday, and you spent the entire day together yesterday," Margie needled. "You know him well enough for a quick smooch."

Jeanie laughed. "Once, I caught Margie necking with some fella she just met!"

"Horsefeathers," Margie said. "He was just whispering in my ear."

"Yeah, that's not what I saw."

Laura laughed, too. "Well, Jax didn't. I'll leave it at that."

"When do we get to meet this Jax Diamond?" Margie asked.

"I already met him at the ballgame," Jeanie told her. "He's a dreamboat."

"If you hadn't stood us up, you could have met him, too, Margie," Laura stated.

"I could never sit through a baseball game, doll. I tried to tell you that." She grabbed the kettle and refilled their coffee cups. "The thought of watching grown men tossing a little ball around sounds as dull as dishwater. Now, sneak me into the backroom of a nightclub, and you couldn't drag me out before dawn."

"You're all talk, Margie," Jeanie scolded. "Two Gin Rickeys and you're blotto. Me, too. You'd never last until sunup. But we both love reading a good detective story. Jax must have a slew of gnarly yarns in his line of work."

"He's in the middle of one right now," Laura said quietly, thinking about it. "He doesn't think Samuel Sanders died of a heart attack."

"Are you on the level?" Jeanie gasped. "Does he think it was murder?"

Laura didn't want to say too much. Everything Jax and Tim had discussed was just speculation right now, as Tim had pointed out. Yet, she was curious to know more about the Robert and Kitty rumors. "Jax just mentioned that he had his suspicions. He did tell me that he was part of the Kitty Cooper investigation. Jeanie, you said that you heard a rumor that Robert Ashworth had an affair with her. Is that true?"

"I don't know for sure."

"I heard the rumors, too," Margie burst in. "And I saw them together once. After rehearsal one day, the girls and I decided to have lunch at the little cafe on Fulton Street. The two of them were sitting at the back corner table. They started arguing about something. Kitty was so mad, she stormed out."

Laura found that strangely coincidental. "When did that happen, Margie?"

"Oh, I don't know. Over the winter some time. It was cold out, that's all I remember. Did they ever find the men who broke into her place?"

"Jax didn't say."

"When are you going to see him again?" Jeanie asked.

"This week some time. I have practice at the theater now, and I'm going to be late if I don't get moving." She gathered her handbag and headed for the door.

"Wait for me, Laura!" Margie called out as she gulped the last of her coffee. "I'll ride the trolley with you part of the way. I have an appointment at the beauty salon. You know, you really should change your hair color, Laura. Men love platinum blondes."

"I wish, Margie. But it wouldn't look half as good on me as it does you and Jeanie."

While they walked to Dekalb Avenue to wait for the trolley, Margie wanted to hear more about her weekend with Jax. Laura told her about seeing the Statue of Liberty for the first time, and how breathtaking it was. And she went on about the fun they had at Coney Island.

"I've been seeing someone, too," Margie admitted as they boarded the trolley.

"Oh, I'm so glad. Who?"

"A bigshot who owns the Cotton Club." Laura looked shocked, so Margie quickly told her, "Don't say anything to Jeanie. You saw how she reacted when I mentioned going to nightclubs. She thinks they're all run by gangsters."

"So do I, Margie!"

"Well, you're too nice to give me a tough time about it. Jeanie would never let me hear the end of it. Besides, he's filthy rich and not a bad looker either."

"I'm surrounded by gold diggers," Laura kidded. But they reached Margie's stop and said their goodbyes.

Laura sat there daydreaming as they journeyed through the heavy street traffic. The trolly started slowing to a crawl. Then, it stopped altogether, and several drivers around them blew their horns. As they sat there at a standstill, a few passengers grew impatient and got off the trolley to walk the rest of the distance. When the driver announced that they would be stuck there for some time, Laura decided to get off, too. Since they had already arrived in Manhattan, the theater was only about nine or ten blocks away.

Yet, the sidewalks were nearly as congested with people rushing in every direction. As she waited to cross the street at the next corner, a chill suddenly ran up her spine, as though someone was watching her. Instinctively, she looked around, but she shrugged it off since everyone was so tightly jammed together, standing shoulder-to-shoulder. When the policeman blew his whistle, she was literally being pushed along with the crowd to the other side of the street.

She broke free of the swarm of people after the next block when she turned down West Forty-Ninth Street. She hurried along, not wanting to be late for practice, but the hair at the nape of her neck bristled with that same feeling again. This time, she didn't even glance behind her. She quickened her stride, and her heart began pounding faster and louder until it nearly drowned the street noise. Thankfully, the theater was only another block away, and she kept her focus straight ahead.

Finally, she reached the theater. She quickly headed down the alley towards the back door and opened it. Only then was she brave enough to turn around. It didn't appear as though anyone had been trailing her. All she saw was a few passersby on the main road. After she inhaled a few deep breaths to relax, she realized that her imagination had gotten away from her.

Inside the theater, Laura noticed everyone was back to work. The hallways were full of performers and the crew, and it felt good to be here again. She greeted everyone and stopped to chat with those she knew well.

Finally, she made her way to her dressing room and stood in the doorway, smiling and glancing around. The room was neat and spotless. The floral bouquets that she'd received had been sent to the nearby hospital, and the room was dusted and mopped with a heavy fresh scent of cedar floor polish. It smelled wonderfully familiar to her. She set her handbag on the chair and pulled off her hat. She tossed it on her dressing table, and her smile left her.

Next to her vanity bag and hand mirror on the table, there was a small glass vase containing one fresh gardenia.

12
The Notepad

Laura snatched her white tunic and pink silk tights, and she disappeared behind her dressing screen to change. Within a few minutes, she heard her door open and peeked out. "Annie! I'm so glad to see you. You didn't have to come to work today, though. It's only practice."

"I needed to escape my grandchildren for a while." She took off her cardigan sweater and hung it on the coat tree. "The little devils wear me out."

Laura had finished dressing and greeted Annie with a loving hug. "You would be lost without them." She wandered over to the vanity. "Annie, you weren't in the dressing room earlier, were you? It seems someone sent one of those pretty flowers again. Still without a card. I was hoping you might have seen who delivered it."

"No, Miss Laura, I just arrived at the theater."

She heard the piano music, which was the casts' signal that practice had begun. She put on her dancing slippers, hurried through the hallway, and joined the others on stage for their warmups. When they pivoted around, she noticed Charley sitting on the piano bench, rather than Mister Beacham. It didn't surprise her overmuch since Mister Beacham had worked at the theater for years and possessed such skill that he wasn't required to attend every practice. Although, she couldn't remember the last time he had missed a rehearsal.

But she was disappointed. Despite everything else, or perhaps because of it, she had hoped to find out if Mister Beacham had given the director his copy of the Songbird manuscript last week.

Two and a half hours later, they were given a fifteen-minute break, and the cast dispersed. Annie stood beside Charley at the piano, handing out clean towels and pouring cups of fresh water for everyone from a large thermos. George Mitchell and Laura wandered over while discussing the first of their practice scenes together, which was scheduled next. Laura thanked Annie, then continued chatting with George while she drank a few cupfuls of water and used the towel to dry the sweat from her neck and hair.

"Miss Laura?" Annie called softly, wiggling her finger and motioning that she wanted to talk with her.

Laura told George that she would see him after the break, and curiously, she followed Annie a few feet away from the others. "What is it?"

Annie scowled as she spoke. "That ragamuffin detective is here again. He is backstage, over there." She pointed in the direction. "He is asking everyone questions now and making a terrible nuisance of himself."

Laura saw Jax talking with Sam, one of the stagehands. He was dressed in the same ugly brown suit, and he stood there holding that annoying pad and pencil while questioning Sam about something. For a second, she started to smile, seeing him here, but that disappeared when she wondered *why* he was here. "Thank you for telling me, Annie."

"He is up to no good, that one," Annie grumbled.

Laura draped the towel around her neck and made her way towards them. Yet, she kept her distance at first, trying to overhear their conversation.

But Jax noticed her there. "Hello." He didn't wait for a reply and turned back to Sam. "So, when the doorman isn't at his post, the first person who walks by accepts the delivery?"

"That's right," Sam said.

"One more question, Sam. Who do you think is the prettiest girl in the cast?"

Sam laughed and walked away.

Jax noticed that Laura was peeking over his shoulder, so he tucked his notepad back into his pocket. "How nice to see you again."

She eyed him suspiciously. "Funny that you failed to mention you were coming here today."

He flashed that sly grin at her. "It was a last-minute decision."

"Hmm. Do you know what else is funny? The page of your notepad was blank. And the tip of your pencil is always sharp."

"You are amazing, Miss Graystone. I grossly underestimated your observation skills."

"There isn't anything written in your notepad, is there?"

"Nope. It's all up here." He tapped his forehead. "For some reason, everything worth remembering seems to stick in my head so I can sift through it later on."

"Really? So, what is the purpose of the notepad?"

"I use it as a tool to make people nervous enough to tell me the truth."

Surprisingly, that made sense since it certainly did that to her. "And what about your rumpled brown suit?" But his expression turned sad as he glanced down at himself. She felt terrible for pointing that out to him, and she was about to apologize when he looked at her again and smirked.

"It makes a suspect think I'm inept," he told her. "Now, you know all my secrets, Miss Graystone."

"Oh, I doubt it, Detective Diamond."

He took a step closer to her. "I watched you practice on stage. You're a very talented dancer."

His tone had softened and his gaze turned intense. So much

so, it took her breath away for a moment.

"Do you like listening to jazz music, Laura?"

"I suppose..."

"You'll probably be too tired tonight, but there's a place I'd love to take you tomorrow night if you're free. I think you'd really enjoy it."

The director called everyone back to practice, and she snapped out of her trance. "Jax, what are you doing here at the theater?"

"I'm trying to find out who delivered Sanders' meal to him the day he died. I haven't had any luck yet. I was also hoping to talk with Robert Ashworth, but no one has seen him today. Do you mind if I stick around for a while and watch?"

"No, not at all." She turned to leave, but he caught her hand.

"You never answered me. Are you free tomorrow night?"

She smiled. "As long as you wear a different suit."

As she made her way back on stage, she couldn't shake the remnants of the hot and cold sensations running through her, a tingling that sent goosebumps up and down her arms and made her light-headed without feeling faint. And it wasn't until she and George began to rehearse their scene together that it dissipated. But as hard as she tried not to let her vision wander towards Jax standing backstage, it seemed her eyes had a mind of their own.

By the time practice was finished, Jax had left, and she went back to her dressing room to change. Annie had laid her street clothes neatly over the screen. After she was finished dressing, she sat at the vanity to brush her hair.

"I saw you talking with the detective," Annie stated.

"Annie, please don't worry. He's really very harmless."

"And charming, too," she added with a giggle as she retrieved her sweater from the coat rack.

Laura couldn't believe her ears and stared at her.

Annie was still smiling. "The Detective and I had a little private chat while you were on stage. I found him to be a very honest and bright young man. He reminds me of my youngest,

Alberto." She went over to hug Laura and told her that she would see her on Wednesday for the performance.

Laura sat there, dazed. Annie was like a brick wall when she met someone new, and it took her forever to warm up to anyone. If she ever did. Only a few hours ago, she had called Jax a ragamuffin right before giving her fair warning that he was backstage. She wondered what on earth Jax could have possibly said to her to turn her around so quickly and completely.

When she was leaving her dressing room, she glanced at the gardenia that Annie had moved to the far shelf, then she shut the door and made her way downstairs. She saw Charley and Jimmy on the stairwell. She called to them, and they waited for her to catch up.

"It was a great practice today," she told them. "I was surprised Mister Beacham didn't show up today. Especially since we had four days off."

"He planned on being here," Charley said. "Something must have come up. I got a phone call from the stage manager this morning asking me to come in. Like Jimmy, I only live a hop, skip, and a jump away, so we're the ones who always get called in last minute."

"Mister Kratz didn't mention why Mister Beacham couldn't make it here today, did he?" But Charley shook his head. "Have you seen or heard from him, Jimmy?"

"No, Miss Graystone. The stage crew had the weekend off, too. I love this place, but not enough to come here on my day off. I think the maintenance crew were the only ones working over the weekend."

They left the theater together. Laura said goodbye to them and headed down the street by herself. The fact that Mister Beacham didn't show up weighed on her mind. They often worked closely together, sometimes after hours, so she knew a great deal about him. He had turned sixty-four last month, and he lived alone, ever since his wife had passed away from pneumonia last year. They never had any children, and sadly, he had no other family. She wished now that she knew where he lived or at least had thought to ask him for his number.

As soon as she settled inside her apartment, she picked up the telephone and dialed zero. When the operator answered, she explained that she needed the number for a co-worker whose last name was Beacham. The operator asked her what city, and when she replied that he lived in New York City, she was told that it was too large of an area. The woman needed a specific county, town, or borough.

Laura hung up the phone realizing that she didn't even know Mister Beacham's first name, let alone what borough he lived in. And she was embarrassed since she knew so many other things about him. She sat there for a moment, then she got up and snatched her handbag. She shuffled through it looking for the card Jax had given her with his telephone number on it.

As she stared at it, she considered calling him, to see if he could find out where Mister Beacham lived. Then, she changed her mind. He couldn't help her any more than the operator with so little information. Besides, she was undoubtedly getting herself worked up over nothing. There was probably a very good reason Mister Beacham wasn't there today, and it really wasn't any of her business.

That's when she blamed her panic on everything that had happened over the weekend. There were a lot of crazy things going on, between Jax's car brakes and seeing Robert Ashworth with Mister Sanders' wife together. Not to mention, someone might have been following them at the amusement park. No wonder she was wound up so tight. She decided what she needed was a nice steamy bubble bath to relax her, and she headed into the bathroom.

Later that night, she relaxed in bed, feeling completely refreshed. All her worries had left her as she watched the brilliant moonlight streaming through her window. It reminded her of Jax, and their walk home last night. But the telephone rang, breaking those thoughts. She threw the covers off and hurried into the other room to answer it.

"Hello?" She smiled when she heard Jax's voice. "Yes, you

woke me up."

He apologized. Then, he told her that Gus had fixed his car, and he would pick her up tomorrow night at six o'clock. Unless she couldn't wait that long to see him again.

She held back a chuckle. "It won't be easy, but I'll try. Good night, Jax." She hung up the phone, went back into the bedroom, still grinning, and comfortably slid under the covers.

13
Hemlock

Tuesday, June 5

The following morning, Jax sat in the outer office, tapping his pencil rapidly on the wooden arm of the chair, with Ace sitting beside him. “Do you know how much longer it’ll be, Gertie? I’ve been waiting over an hour.”

The grey-haired woman slowly glanced up at him. “You know Lieutenant Simmons is a busy man, Detective Diamond. He’ll be with you as soon as he is free. Would you mind refraining from strumming your pencil? I have a heavy workload, too, and it’s distracting.”

“Sorry.” He stood up and started pacing the small room, humming to himself.

Irritably, Gertie picked up the telephone, called the Lieutenant on the intercom, and reminded him that Jax was still waiting. “Yes, sir.” She expelled a loud sigh of relief, and announced, “He will see you now.”

Jax thanked her, grabbed his hat on the chair, and he and Ace entered the adjoining room. “I appreciate you seeing me on such short notice, Lieutenant.”

He greeted them both and offered Jax a seat. “I’m not sure how I can help you. Gertie said it had something to do with the

Kitty Cooper investigation. We closed that case months ago."

"I wasn't aware that you could close an unsolved murder."

The Lieutenant sat down behind his desk. "It depends upon the case. Now, why did you want to see me?"

Jax pulled out his notepad and flipped through it. "I came upon some information recently that I'm hoping will convince you to reopen the investigation."

"Hearsay is a far cry from evidence, Jax. You know that as well as I do from your time on the force. Unless you have something more substantial, I'm afraid..."

"Just hear me out, Lieutenant," Jax insisted.

Lieutenant Simmons leaned back in his chair and motioned for him to proceed.

"I know you questioned and dismissed a couple of prime suspects. Did you know that during the months leading up to Kitty Cooper's murder, she was secretly involved with a prominent gentleman in the city?"

"From what I heard, there were a few of them. Who would you be referring to?"

Jax noticed the irritation in the other man's voice and stared down at his notepad, hesitant to answer. Lieutenant Simmons had been his superior when he worked on the force, and he had every respect for the man, on the job and off. He was also a stickler for dotting every i and crossing every t. So, Jax braced himself for the repercussion that was sure to follow. He took a deep breath, lifted his head, and looked at the man directly.

"Robert Ashworth," he said quietly. But surprisingly, the Lieutenant didn't respond the way Jax thought he would. In fact, he didn't seem very surprised or angry with the accusation. He simply sat there, contemplating it. Then, he stood up, walked around to the front of the desk, and leaned against it.

"Did you read the file?" the Lieutenant asked.

"Yes, sir. It stated that you questioned Mister Ashworth at the time, yet only about Miss Cooper's work ethics, along with her comings and goings at the theater on the day of her death. Was that the extent of your inquiries?"

"Not exactly. Robert never admitted knowing Miss Cooper personally, but I ran across some documents that proved the woman's luxury apartment on West 57th Street was funded through Ashworth's bank. The same with receipts for her jewelry and furs from Bloomingdale's, and Lord and Taylor. Before I had time to pinpoint exactly which bank account the money was withdrawn from, the captain called off the investigation, collected all the evidence I'd gathered, and closed the case."

"Just like that?"

"Between you and me, Jax. I think the Ashworths paid the captain or the mayor plenty to keep Robert's involvement from going public. And there wasn't anything I could do about it."

"Maybe you couldn't back then. But I think Robert Ashworth had something to do with Samuel Sanders' death. I know the medical examiner determined it was natural causes, but I don't think so, sir."

"Going on one of your hunches again, Jax?"

"It's more than a hunch. I was the first person on the scene, and there are too many discrepancies for the man to have suddenly had a heart attack. I think Robert Ashworth and Sanders' wife conspired to kill him because she couldn't obtain a divorce. If Robert Ashworth was capable of murdering Kitty Cooper or paying someone else to do it, he is certainly capable of killing his current girlfriend's husband. I know for a fact that he's involved with Missus Sanders."

It took the Lieutenant a minute to respond. Finally, he reached over to pet Ace. "I didn't want either of you leaving the force, Jax. You've been right more than you've been wrong. And Tim hasn't been happy with any of his partners since you and Ace left. Are you sure you don't want to re-enlist?"

Jax laughed. "Not at the moment, sir, but thanks. So, what happens now?"

"Off the record, keep investigating this. Discreetly, please. It won't help my standing with Captain Ryan if word got out. I assume you shared your hunch with Tim. I'm fine with him helping you as long it stays between you. But keep me informed.

I'll see that the city pays you if you produce anything substantial. There's nothing I'd like better than to see Robert Ashworth behind bars if he's guilty."

"Thank you, sir." He shook the Lieutenant's hand and left.

Tim was waiting for him in the office area. "Good morning, Jax."

"Speak of the devil."

"I probably don't want to know what you were talking with the Lieutenant about, do I?" Tim asked.

"Probably not. What are your plans for the day?"

"I have a feeling you already know."

Jax laughed. "Let's take my car, and I'll fill you in."

"I'd rather drive my patrol car."

"You sound paranoid, Murph. Old Nellie is less conspicuous."

"And mine is a heck of a lot safer."

As Jax drove to Manhattan, he explained to Tim that he had every intention of asking Robert Ashworth a few indirect questions at the theater yesterday. He'd hoped to find out if Ashworth was present at the theater when Sanders' meal was delivered last Tuesday. And hopefully, trick Ashworth into telling him about his relationship with Patricia Sanders. He wanted proof that the two of them had hooked up before Sander's death. Otherwise, it merely looked like he was consoling the widow of his former employee after the fact.

But now that he knew the murders were connected, and the captain had shut down the Kitty Cooper investigation, they had to be careful not to alert the Ashworths that they had unofficially reopened it. Which meant they couldn't request any financial documentations from the Ashworths' bank, Kitty Cooper's apartment building, or receipts from the high-end department stores. Yet, they could easily and casually ask the store clerks, desk clerks, and bellhops a few questions.

So, Jax and Tim spent the day at Bloomingdales, and Lord and Taylors, where they discovered that Robert Ashworth had been a frequent customer since last Christmas. He'd spent an exorbitant amount of money in both the women's clothing and coat departments, as well as their jewelry departments. Finally, they ended up at the 57th Street Apartments. Curiously here, everyone seemed tight-lipped about any goings-on during Kitty Cooper's stay in the penthouse.

Except for one elevator operator who admitted receiving very generous tips from Robert Ashworth, asking him not to pick up any other passengers whenever he rode the elevator to the penthouse.

"Well, we found out a lot about the man today," Tim said as Jax drove them back to the station house just south of the Williamsburg Bridge. "But what good is it if Captain Ryan won't re-open the investigation?"

"We just keep digging and collecting evidence until we have enough to change his mind. You haven't told me what you think of Laura yet, Murph. She's quite a gal, isn't she? When I was at the theater yesterday, I watched her on stage. Her singing is incredible with such rich tones and a wide pitch range. I'd bet my last buck that she reached at least four octaves perfectly. I've never heard anything so beautiful."

"You're carrying a real torch for her already, aren't you? Carla and I like her a lot, but no offense, Jax. We think she's way out of your league."

Jax smiled. "I know. Isn't that terrific?"

"It is if you're setting yourself up for a big fall. According to Carla, Laura is a rising star, and she's going to make it big time. You and I know better than anyone that the Broadway scene is a far cry from our humble lives."

"You're a real stick in the mud, Murph."

"Okay, then let's talk about the person who followed you at Coney Island."

"Like I said, it was my imagination," Jax returned flatly. He regretted saying anything to Tim about it in the first place since it had nothing at all to do with this case or any other.

For a while, he'd just had a feeling of being followed as he and Laura walked to different rides at the park. An inexplicably weird feeling that seemed ridiculous given the massive crowd.

Then, when his horse reached the finish line during the steeple-chase, he saw a man standing behind Laura. Someone from his past. And it startled him since he'd heard the person had died eight years ago.

When he noticed Ace chasing after the man, Jax still wondered if they'd been followed, but he realized that his eyes must have been playing tricks on him as to who the man was. Since he didn't want to get into all of that with Tim, he decided to just drop the issue altogether. And he was glad Tim fell silent.

Jax pulled his car up to the curb. "I have to go home and get all dolled-up now, Murph. I have a date with my rising star tonight."

Tim laughed and got out of the car. "I'll see you tomorrow, Jax."

Ace jumped into the front seat while Jax waited for a few cars to go by. Then, he pulled the car out into the road. But within seconds, Ace started barking. Jax slowed down to find out why, and he heard Tim shouting for him to stop. He slammed on the brakes, nearly getting hit from behind, and he held up traffic until Tim nudged Ace out of the way and jumped back into the car.

"Stan just told me that Doctor Norris called. He wants me to stop by his office as soon as possible. I figured you'd want to come, too."

"You bet I do."

They headed north to First Avenue in Manhattan and entered the medical examiner's building. Doctor Norris greeted them and introduced Doctor Gettler, the chief toxicologist. Doctor Gettler explained that he'd spent the past few weeks in Europe. Upon his return Sunday night, he and Doctor Norris worked together to re-examine the specimens Joe had collected in Samuel Sanders' apartment.

"I told Doctor Gettler that you had questioned whether there were any poisonous substances that were still undetectable, Detective," Doctor Norris said. "Unfortunately, there are too many, and I lost quite a bit of sleep thinking about it that night. Isolating and identifying toxic structures of chemical compounds have been challenging enough. Especially since Mayor Hylan openly ridicules our work and cut the funding necessary for us to continue. So much so, I have been contributing my own money to further our research."

"What did you find?" Jax asked anxiously.

"Joe mentioned that cyanosis, a blueish tint to the skin, had already developed when he examined Mister Sanders," the Doctor told him. "While that is an inevitable part of the decomposing process, it would in itself tell me that the man had died eight to twelve hours earlier. But Joe also mentioned the overheated temperature in the apartment, and that would greatly accelerate the process, which is why I was so firm in my initial diagnosis. Yet, cyanosis is also the first sign of poison ingestion. In hindsight, I should not have dismissed the concept so completely."

"Due to limited funds, we have only recently begun working on isolating plant compounds," Doctor Gettler added. "And we did, indeed, come across a small trace of cicutoxin, a naturally-occurring poisonous compound produced by several plants from the Apiaceae family. The first isolation of pure cicutoxin was confirmed a few years ago after twenty-seven similar cases of illness had been reported, with twenty-one resulting in death."

"So, in laymen's terms, there was poison in his food?"

Doctor Norris nodded. "Cicutoxin has been found in a few species of hemlock plants, which grow wild and are often mistaken for edible roots such as wild parsnip, celery, turnips, and carrots. The toxin is present throughout the plant, but the root carries the highest concentration. Ingestion of a mere two-centimeter portion of the root could be fatal for an adult."

"Wild parsnips and carrots?" Jax asked. "The waiter at L'Aiglon Restaurant mentioned their chicken and biscuit dish had those vegetables in it. But even though they look similar in appearance, wouldn't someone be able to taste the difference? I would think a poisonous plant would taste bad or bitter?"

"On the contrary. The root of the plant emits a scent similar to fresh turnips, and they possess quite a sweet flavor," Doctor Gettler replied.

14
Duke's Club

Jax and Tim left the medical examiner's building and sat silently in his car. Even though Jax had been convinced all along that Sanders' death was a homicide, they both needed time to fully grasp it.

"I've got to report this to Captain Ryan," Tim stated.

"Inform Lieutenant Simmons, too. This gives us reason to start openly questioning suspects like Patricia Sanders and Robert Ashworth, but only regarding Sanders' death. The Lieutenant warned me that Captain Ryan won't listen to anything having to do with Kitty Cooper's murder. Not without solid evidence as good as this."

"Jax, this proves Sanders was murdered, and we know the poison was in his dinner. But it seems far-fetched that Sanders' wife and Ashworth killed him. Going from filing for divorce to murder is pretty extreme."

"Maybe. Sam Sanders had the number of his wife's lawyer in

his desk drawer, so it's reasonable to assume that he'd found out about his wife wanting a divorce. Maybe he knew about their affair too. Ashworth could have been worried that he'd go public about it, tarnishing his impeccable reputation and family name. The man was bold enough to pay someone in the city plenty to keep his relationship with Kitty Cooper off the records."

"But to kill the man in such a sinister way? That was a slow and agonizing death."

"Yeah, but not as messy and obvious as a gun or knife. If it weren't for Doctors Norris and Gettler, they would have gotten away with it. I agree, though. This isn't going to be easy to prove."

"Don't you have a date tonight?"

Jax sat up. "What time is it?"

"Going on six-thirty."

"Dang." He quickly started the car and headed back to the station house. "She's not going to be very happy with me for being late."

"I suppose you want me to give her a call and let her know you'll be there soon?"

"You're a peach, Murph. Thanks."

After dropping Tim off, Jax raced through the streets to get home, at least as fast as Old Nellie would get him there. He cleaned up, filled Ace's food and water bowl, then headed out the door. But he passed right by his car at the curb and ran down the street in the opposite direction of Laura's apartment building. He knew Missus Kirby, a sweet old widow, had set up her flower cart just around the block. He handed her a dollar for half a dozen red roses and told her to keep the change. The woman wrapped a satin ribbon around the stems, he waved his thanks and rushed back to his car.

Shortly after seven-thirty, he stood on Laura's doorstep. He took a deep breath and knocked. As soon as Laura opened the door, he immediately began apologizing to her for being late, but he stopped mid-sentence when he saw her. She was wearing a shimmering pink evening gown with an uneven hemline that fell above her ankles, and a sparkling pearl headband. He had never seen anyone look so radiant.

She smiled. "It was thoughtful of you to have Tim call me."

Slowly, he handed her the flower, but he was speechless.

"Thank you. Did you want to come in?" she asked.

He followed her into the apartment. "Did Tim tell you why I'm late?"

"He said it pertained to work." She pulled out a porcelain vase from the kitchen cupboard, set the roses inside, and filled it with water.

He kept his eyes on her. "The medical examiner finally confirmed that Sam Sanders' death was a homicide. He found a trace of poison in his system. It's a whole different ballgame now."

"So, you were right all along. I was still hoping it wasn't true, for Mister Sanders' sake." She set the vase on the coffee table in the living room and approached him.

"Let's not talk about it tonight," he told her. "I was thinking about taking you to a place where I spend a lot of time, but now, I'm losing my nerve."

She gazed up at him. "Jax, take me someplace fun. All I've done is work on stage since I came to the city. Sunday was the best time I've ever had."

He wanted to kiss her then. If Tim's statement about her being out of his league wasn't so heavy on his mind, and he didn't think that he'd scare her off, he would have. He couldn't remember the last time he enjoyed spending time with someone else. Maybe never. There was so much trash sitting in his head, from his childhood right through to working on the police force. And he's been struggling to let go of it.

He realized then that the past few years he's been hiding away, burying his head in the sand as though the memories of his past would all magically disappear when he emerged. But it was always there. During his entire life, he's had only two loves. Ace, and what he was about to introduce to her now.

He offered her his arm. "Then, it's settled. I had a great day with you, too, so I'm taking you to the one place I enjoy most of all." He escorted her to his car and drove through Manhattan. But the closer they got to their destination, the more nervous he became. "I know there are plenty of nightclubs here in your territory, but there are a few places just north of Manhattan. The Pelican Club is new and one of the more popular places. But the proprietor, Orin Marino, and I don't get along so well."

"Why not?"

"Like most of the nightclub owners, he's a known bootlegger and racketeer who can't seem to keep his nose out of trouble. While the Pelican Club is all about booze. Duke's Club is all about good music. I figure that's right up your alley."

Laura was more than curious now. And her puzzlement heightened after Jax parked the car and told her they had a short walk. Yet rather than head down the street, they entered Roy's Shoe Store on the corner. Jax held her hand as they passed by racks of men, women, and children's shoes into the back room. There, he led her down a dark, narrow stairway and through the corridor to the last door.

When it opened, Jax greeted the attendant, and the man motioned for them to go inside. Laura looked around in amazement. The dim lighting and smokiness lingering in the air made it difficult to see the entire cabaret-style room. Yet, it was filled with people from all walks of life dressed from casual to elegant, and the room was lavishly decorated with red wallpaper and gold-framed portraits. There was a bar, a few dozen tables, and a dancefloor. But it was the quartet playing on stage who gripped her attention.

Jax pointed to the table near the band, and as they walked through the crowd, everyone they passed acknowledged him. After they sat down, he leaned over and asked, "I'm going to wait a while to have a cocktail, but I can order you one."

She shook her head, still focused on the musicians. Everyone in the room remained quiet, too, as they listened to the band. Laura was familiar with diverse types of music, including Dixieland, swing, and bebop. But she found jazz particularly interesting since it made the best use of brass and woodwind instruments and, her specialty, the piano. She also enjoyed the improvisation, syncopation, and rhythm. Yet, hearing it and seeing it in person was a whole new experience altogether.

"Is this place all right with you?" Jax asked when the quartet stopped playing for a short break.

"It's perfect. Thank you for bringing me here."

"Well, hang onto that thought," he chuckled. As the band passed by their table, they each stopped to talk with Jax, and he introduced them to Laura.

"You must come here a lot," she told him after they left. "You know everyone."

He looked around, smiling. "It's like a second home to me."

"You surprise me, Jax. From Coney Island to this. It's like night and day."

"Well, this club is as illegal as the rest of the nightclubs, but there hasn't been any trouble here, so the police leave this place alone. What I admire is that every penny the owner makes from the booze they sell is generously given to the employees and the band, rather than overstuffing his own pocket. That's not customary at other nightclubs, which is why they're often raided."

She was about to respond, but he suddenly stood up.

"Would you mind terribly if I left you here alone for a few minutes?" he asked. "I won't be far away."

"No, that's fine."

He stood there a moment longer. "Don't go anywhere."

The band had gathered back on stage again, and curiously, she watched Jax join them. One of the band members pointed to the black case on the floor. She wondered what was going on when she saw Jax open the case and lift a brass trumpet from its berth. He blew through the mouthpiece a few times and walked over to stand beside the saxophone player.

She threw herself back into her chair, stunned, yet smiling and laughing at the same time in disbelief. The entire band played a few warmup notes, then they began another tune.

During the next half hour, Laura didn't move, and she could barely breathe as she watch Jax play. Not once did he need to even glance at a sheet of music. What he hadn't memorized was expertly improvised. And if he wasn't looking at her, his eyes were closed, visibly feeling the overwhelming elation that she always did while singing or playing the piano.

She couldn't take her eyes off him, especially when each musician took turns with a brief solo. Jax played the trumpet with his heart and soul, to the point where she could feel him taking himself away from the crowd and the room to a place so far beyond anyone's reach.

When the tune ended, he walked to the back of the stage to pack his trumpet into the case. The band members were disappointed that he was finished, and he kept shaking his head, letting them know he was done. Before joining her again, he motioned to the bartender, and immediately, a beer and a Gin Rickey were delivered to their table. And he held that dimpled grin on her as he sat down. But it appeared more humble than smug to her now, as though he was nervous to hear what she thought.

"Did I do okay?" he asked.

"Okay? Jax, that was wonderful. I can't even think of a word to describe it. Where on earth did you learn to play the trumpet, and why didn't you say something? You are unbelievably talented. I was starstruck."

"Starstruck, eh? Well, that's way more than I expected, given your abilities. I don't mean that in a negative way. I mean..."

She reached over and placed her hand on his. "I know what you're saying. Thank you so much for introducing this part of yourself to me."

He turned his hand around and folded his fingers around hers. "It feels good being able to share it with someone else for once."

It was well past midnight by the time Jax drove Laura home and walked her to the door of her apartment. She retrieved the keys from her purse, but he took them and opened the door for her. She turned to him. "Did you want to come in?"

He rested his hand on the wall beside her. "No, not tonight. It's late, and I should be getting home to Ace."

His blue eyes gripped her again. "I loved watching you play."

"Not as much as I love watching you sing. My little bag of tricks is empty now. No more surprises."

She smiled. "I'm sure you have a few more up your sleeve."

"Yeah, maybe. Well, I guess I should go."

She headed into her apartment, then looked back at him. "If your coffee is as good as your lamb chops, I could stop by before I go to the theater tomorrow morning. Ace probably misses me anyway."

"I make the best dang coffee in the city."

15
The Suspects

Wednesday, June 6

"Ace, relax. She'll be here soon," Jax called from the kitchen when he saw Ace sitting by the front door. "I never should have told you that she was coming over." But Ace didn't budge. "I guess I can't blame you for being anxious." And he went back to prepping breakfast.

A few minutes later, Ace stood by the door, wagging his tail, even before Laura knocked. Jax hurried over to open it, but Ace budged him aside to greet her first. "Good morning," she laughed, and she bent down to hug Ace.

Jax snatched her hand, shooing Ace away, and led her into the kitchen. "I hope you're hungry."

"I usually just have coffee in the morning, Jax. I didn't expect you to cook anything."

"Once you taste my puff pancakes with homemade raspberry jam, you'll be back for more."

As they ate breakfast, Jax asked Laura what she had planned for the day. She told him that she had a few errands to run this morning, then she, Jeanie, and Margie were going to meet for lunch and do a little window shopping.

"I met Jeanie at the ballgame, didn't I? She's a pretty woman."

"Margie is, too. She's Jeanie's roommate. She was supposed to join us for the game, but she doesn't like baseball very much. She's anxious to meet you, though."

"What time do you need to be at the theater for your performance tonight?" he asked.

"Four o'clock for rehearsal. I'll probably get there a little earlier." But her mind drifted. "Margie told me that she's been seeing the owner of the Cotton Club. I'm not sure who that is, but after what you said last night about club owners being bootleggers and racketeers, I'm worried about her."

"With good reason," he said. "Tell her to be careful, Laura. We don't need another Butterfly murder on our hands."

"Oh, Jax, don't scare me. I'll make sure I talk with her about it this afternoon. Okay, enough of me. I want to hear what you have planned for your day now that you've got proof Mister Sanders' death was a homicide."

"Murph has the pleasure of informing Patricia Sanders of our findings and asking her a few questions, hopefully making her nervous enough to say something she shouldn't. I have a more grueling task. I'm going to pay the Ashworths a little surprise visit at their home. As the owner of the theater, Missus Ashworth needs to be notified that we're investigating a murder now, and I'm curious to watch her son's reaction when told of it."

"Margie said New York City was a far cry from my little hometown, but I never realized how true that was until all this happened. I still can't believe that Robert Ashworth could be involved in two murders. And you think he paid someone to cut your brake cables, too, don't you? I haven't wanted to even think about that. We both could have been killed."

"Thanks to your ingenuity, we weren't, Laura. And whoever was responsible didn't know that you would be in the car with me, so you're not in any danger."

"But you are," she said worriedly.

"It's nice having someone worry about me. But between you, Ace and Murph, I'm as snug as a bug."

"Well, I don't envy you today. I shouldn't say anything negative against Missus Ashworth after everything she's done for my career, but she's a very dramatic, self-absorbed woman. Of course, given her wealth, I suppose that's to be expected."

His eyes lit up. "Why don't you come with me?"

She burst out laughing and stood up. "You're on your own, Detective. Thank you for breakfast. It was delicious. I'm going to leave while the getting's good."

An hour later, Jax and Ace headed for the Ashworth mansion on Fifth Avenue. Laura's comments didn't help his nerves any. As it was, he had to tread ever so carefully with the Ashworths, Robert especially. He needed to pose every question without sounding accusatory. Otherwise, they would become defensive and resort to using their money and influence to stop the investigation, just as they had done in the Kitty Cooper case.

"Unbelievable..." Jax muttered as he pulled up across the street from the Ashworth mansion. "How would you like to live in that joint, Ace?"

The fifty-seven-room stone mansion spanned the entire block with a nine-foot cast iron barricade guarding the estate from trespassers. While Jax sat there studying the palace and the surroundings, he didn't see Robert's Rolls-Royce. But curiously, he noticed Sanders' sporty Fiat out front, along with a turquoise Pierce-Arrow parked behind it, which was another lavish vehicle that cost more than his apartment building.

He sat there for a while, silently running through his questions. He wasn't sure if he was prepared to confront both Ashworths and Patricia Sanders at the same time. He also resented the fact that he had to do Tim's dirty work, too, since was supposed to question Patricia at her apartment.

He took a few deep breaths and got out of his car. After he crossed the street, he noticed the front gate had been left open. He climbed the steps and used the brass door knocker to alert those inside. It took the elderly butler exactly eight seconds to answer."

"I need to speak with Missus Ashworth," Jax stated.

"I am sorry, sir, but she traveled to her summer home this

morning."

"Is Mister Ashworth available?" he asked.

"And you are..."

"Detective Diamond. It's an important police matter."

"Wait here, and I will see if he is available."

The butler began closing the door, but Jax stuck his foot out to stop it from shutting. "I'll tell you what. Why don't I wait inside while you find out?" And he boldly entered the domed entryway, ignoring the displeasure on the older man's face.

Reluctantly, the butler turned around. "If you insist, sir, then I must ask you to wait in the library." He led the way to the main hall and headed for the door on their right.

As Jax followed him, he glanced around. The massive foyer was lined with sculpted busts and oil paintings of either their ancestors or other notable people. It was a pretty gruesome scene in his mind. But to each his own, he figured. There were also seven doorways encompassing the room, along with a wide, winding staircase, and an elaborate crystal chandelier hanging from the high ceiling.

As he absorbed every detail around him, he heard voices coming from the room on the opposite side. The butler opened the door to the library, told him to have a seat, and closed the door. Jax waited all of eight seconds before he opened the door again and peeked around. He could still hear people talking across the way. So, when he was assured that the path was clear, he quietly walked through the foyer until he stood just outside the other door. And he found himself staring at a portrait of old Missus Ashworth.

But it was the voices inside the room that held his attention.

"How many times do I have to tell you, Hoffman," Robert yelled. "I don't know anything about a manuscript! Even if I did, Sam's death voids the contracts he signed with the Globe Theater and with us. So basically, it's finders, keepers, as they say."

"I paid a thousand dollars up front for that manuscript," another man shouted. "And I either want that or the money back to me by tomorrow. Otherwise, my lawyer will be contacting your lawyers since I have proof of that payment. Dead or not, your girlfriend is responsible for her husband's debts, including this."

The door flew open, and Jax thanked his lucky stars that he was on the back side of it, hiding there like a thief. The other man stormed out and in his angry, determined stride towards the exit, he never noticed Jax standing there in plain sight.

As soon as the man slammed the front door shut, Jax high-tailed it back to the library as fast as he could. And he sat in the chair contemplating what had just passed and smiling because he'd gotten a good look at Robert's adversary.

Finally, the butler joined him again. "I am sorry, sir, but Mister Ashworth had another pressing matter to attend to. I could certainly have him telephone you when he is available."

Jax stood up, practically smirking. "Why don't you tell him to call Lieutenant Simmons at the thirteenth precinct. It's regarding a murder investigation, so let Mister Ashworth know that it *is* important." And he strolled away.

He climbed down the front steps and as expected, the fancy Pierce-Arrow vehicle had disappeared while Sanders' Fiat was about a block down the road. He laughed out loud as he joined Ace. "Rich folks think they're so smart, Ace, but they aren't half as smart as us, that's for sure."

He was still smiling when he arrived at the precinct and found Tim at his desk. "You had an easy day, didn't you? I'm out there pounding the streets while you're lounging behind your desk."

"Patricia Sanders wasn't home, Jax," Tim squawked. "What was I supposed to do, travel the city looking for her?"

"Sit down, Murph. You're not going to believe this. Conveniently, she was at the Ashworth's mansion. And boy, let me tell you, that place is enormous! I've never seen..."

"Okay, okay, what happened?"

Jax pulled a chair over from another desk and sat down. "While I was waiting to talk to Ashworth, I heard people arguing, and I was able to get close enough to hear what they were saying. Patricia Sanders was in the room, too. Does the name Hoffman sound familiar? He has something to do with Broadway."

"Ben Hoffman, the owner of Globe Theater?"

"You hit the nail on the head. I heard him tell Ashworth that he paid Sam Sanders a thousand bucks for a manuscript. That's the exact amount of dough we found in Sanders' desk drawer. So, it was in payment for the new manuscript he wrote, the one I couldn't find any trace of that night. Hoffman said that he had a signed contract for the rights to that manuscript, and if he didn't get the script or his money back by tomorrow, he was calling his lawyer."

"Hang on, Jax. You're saying Hoffman threatened to get his lawyer involved over some music composition?"

Jax was all fired up. He got out of his chair and started pacing. "I'm not done. At first, Ashworth claimed that he didn't know about the manuscript. Then, he told Hoffman that with Sanders' death, all contracts were null and void. So, it was a matter of finders, keepers. Those were his exact words, Murph. Finders, keepers."

"What did Ashworth say when you questioned him?"

"I didn't. The butler told me that he had another pressing matter and couldn't see me, so I left." Jax sat back down in the chair. "But Ashworth has that manuscript. I'd bet on it. And that puts him, or whoever he paid to do his dirty work, smack dab in Sanders' apartment that night. We know someone took the original. Murph, that manuscript is Ashworth's motive for murdering Sam Sanders."

Tim started laughing. "You're crazy. Do you know how much the Ashworth's are worth? They have more dough than we'll ever see in a lifetime. A thousand dollars is like peanuts to them. How can some Broadway play be motive for murder?"

"That was just a small down payment. If that play becomes a success, which it would with Laura singing the lead, then they would rake in well over a million dollars. Is that enough motive?"

Tim's eyes popped open. "A million?"

"My guess is, Ashworth knew that Sanders had signed a contract with Hoffman, so he had no other choice but to kill him to get that play. It's been driving me crazy trying to figure out what happened to the original."

"But how do we prove that he has it?"

Jax leaned back. "If Hoffman gets his money back tomorrow, or the manuscript, we know Ashworth is guilty. I'll have a little talk with Hoffman about it tomorrow afternoon. He shouldn't have any qualms about opening up to me once he finds out that we have his money here at the station house. But until then, let's get a court order started so we can search the Ashworth mansion and Patricia Sanders' apartment in case that doesn't get us anywhere."

"Didn't you say Sanders wrote that play for Laura?"

Jax smirked, remembering how she grew so flustered when he had asked her that question. "He wrote it with her in mind for the lead," he corrected. But his smile suddenly left him. "Murph, there are two other people who have a copy of that manuscript. That shouldn't matter, should it?"

"Not if Ashworth has the original," Tim told him.

"But what if Ashworth knows there are two copies? What if he worries that Ben Hoffman will try to get his hands on those?"

"Who has the copies?"

"Laura, and some piano player at the Ambassador."

16
The Piano Player

On stage, Laura fumbled during rehearsal a few times, which rarely happened. It began to irritate the other performers, and even the director stopped to stare at her. But she couldn't concentrate and kept glancing over at Charlie playing the piano. The rehearsal was nearly over, and their Wednesday night performance was going to begin in just over an hour. But still, Mister Beacham hadn't shown up.

She noticed the stage manager standing in the hallway. She kept her eyes on him while waiting for the director to dismiss the performers. Then, she hurried off the stage. "Mister Kratz, could I speak with you for a moment?" He turned around. "I'm sorry to trouble you, but do you know where Mister Beacham is? He missed practice the other day, and he isn't here yet. I wondered if you've heard from him?"

"He called the theater on Monday morning and said he needed to go out of town for a few days to visit his sister. He should be back for the next performance on Friday."

"His sister?" she asked. That didn't make any sense. "He told me that he didn't have any other family."

Mister Kratz shrugged. "I don't know, that's what he said.

Maybe it's a sister that he wished he didn't have. I've got two of those." And the man headed down the hallway.

Laura stood there. Something was wrong. She knew for a fact that Mister Beacham didn't have a sister. At least not living. He had told her that both his and his wife's entire families were killed in Romania during the war, but the two of them had miraculously escaped, and they eventually found safe passage to America.

Laura didn't know what to do. "Mister Kratz, wait up!" she yelled as she ran after him. "Do you know where Mister Beacham lives? I'm probably overreacting. You know how melodramatic women can be." She feigned a chuckle. "But I'd feel better if I could ask a friend of mine to check with Mister Beacham's landlord to make sure everything is all right." He obviously wasn't very happy with her request, so she added, "It would really help me to relax so I don't make any mistakes during our performance tonight."

"He lives at the brownstone on Lafayette Avenue," he said abruptly before walking away.

That was only a street over from where she lived. She rushed into her dressing room and found Annie there, waiting for her. "I need a big favor, Annie." She sifted through her handbag and gave her Jax's card. "Would you be a dear and call Jax for me?"

"Of course," she replied.

"Tell him that I need him to check on someone. I'll write down the name and address for you to give to him. I hate to trouble you or him, but I don't know what else to do. If I didn't have this performance, I would go there myself."

"What has you so upset, Miss Laura?"

"I'm hoping it's nothing," she replied, but while she quickly wrote the information down, someone knocked on the door. Annie answered it, and Jax stood there. "Oh, Jax. I'm glad you're here." Laura grabbed the paper and gave it to him. "Mister Beacham, the piano player I told you about, hasn't shown up this week, and that's not like him at all."

"I wondered about him, too, Miss Laura," Annie said. "He has been with the theater for six years now, and I do not believe that he has ever missed a practice or a performance."

"That's what I thought, Annie. Mister Kratz, the stage manager, said that Mister Beacham had called him on Monday, and said that he was going to visit his sister out of town for a few days." She looked up at him. "But he doesn't have any family, Jax. I'm sure of it. I feel bad putting you out like this. Would you mind going to his apartment? He lives right around the corner from both of us. If he isn't there, I don't know what to make of it. But maybe the landlord can confirm that he went on a holiday or something. It would mean so much to me."

He smiled at her reassuringly. "Relax, Laura. I don't mind check it out at all, but I'm sure everything is fine." He left the dressing room, and Tim was waiting for him in the hallway. "Mister Beacham, the piano player hasn't shown up at the theater. He may have gone out of town for a few days, but Laura is pretty worried about him."

"With good reason if he has a copy of that manuscript."

"Stay with Laura, Murph. I'm going to his apartment to see what I can find. And don't upset Laura more by mentioning anything about the manuscript."

"Maybe I should go with you."

"I've got Ace. Just keep an eye on Laura."

Jax easily found the brownstone apartments on Layfette Avenue. He took Ace with him and climbed the front steps. He saw Horace Beacham's name and apartment number, but the front door was locked. He pressed the corresponding buzzer to the man's apartment several times. When that failed, he glanced down the list again, and luckily, the apartment manager's buzzer was the last one.

Within a few minutes, a man around Jax's age, mid-twenties, came to the door. Jax explained who he was, and his reason for being there. The man noticed Ace sitting obediently beside Jax. Just then, Ace stood up and started wagging his tail.

"Nice looking pooch," the man said. "Friendly, too, it looks like."

"He sure is."

The manager reached down to pet him. He allowed them both to enter the building and walked them down the hallway. "I usually don't pay attention to tenants' comings and goings. But ever since Horace's wife died, I've tried to keep an eye on him. He reminds me of my grandfather." He stopped in front of the second last door and searched his keychain. "I realized that I didn't see Horace yesterday, so I took a quick peek into his apartment when he didn't answer the door. Everything looked in order, so I assumed he'd taken a trip somewhere."

"He very well may have," Jax replied. "But he never mentioned going anywhere to his friend at the theater, which seemed strange to her. Thanks for letting us take a look around."

"Of course. Would you mind locking up when you're finished? My wife and I are eating supper right now. And let me know if you hear from him."

Jax thanked him and went inside. As the manager said, everything looked in order. It was a small, one-bedroom apartment, neat and organized. "Well, let's start looking, Ace."

They both wandered around the living area. Jax flipped through the books laying on the end table next to the sofa and checked inside the drawer. He lifted the sofa and chair cushions and got on his knees to search underneath both. Then, he scanned the few books stacked on the shelf in the corner. As he and Ace made their way into the adjoining room, Jax straightened the landscape painting hanging on the wall.

In the kitchen, he opened the icebox. It was nearly empty with only a bottle of milk, a little basket of brown eggs, and something wrapped in a paper bag that smelled like cheese. He opened the two drawers just beneath the counter and inspected the four cupboards above it. The first cupboard contained two plates, two drinking glasses, and two coffee mugs. The second cupboard stored the non-perishables, a loaf of bread, a chunk of butter, and a few cans of beans. The remaining cupboards were empty.

When he found nothing of importance, he noticed Ace had

already gone into the bedroom, so he followed along. It was no bigger than the narrow kitchen. And it only consisted of a single bed and a small chest of drawers. He opened the first drawer and it was as sparse as the icebox, with only a few personal items of clothing. There were three folded shirts and two pairs of trousers in the second drawer. But it was the third and last drawer that he found interesting.

This drawer was so jampacked with articles of clothing that he could barely get it open. And when he finally did, he pulled out each one and discovered that they were women's blouses, full-length skirts, and house dresses. He assumed they belonged to the man's wife.

Ace was standing behind him, and he started barking at the bed. Jax stuffed the clothes back into the drawer. "What did you find, Ace?" He threw the bedcovers aside, but he didn't see anything.

Ace continued barking, then he jumped up on the bed, and using his snout, he tried to move the pillow away. Jax lifted it and saw an oval gold locket necklace underneath. He picked it by the chain to take a closer look. The initials KC were engraved on the front of the locket. "Good work, Ace."

After he closed and locked the door, he walked a few steps down the hall and knocked on the manager's door. "I'm sorry to disturb you again. I wanted to let you know that I didn't find anything that alerted me to Mister Beacham's whereabouts. But I wondered. Would you happen to know what his wife's name was? I'm thinking I might try to find out if they had any family who I could contact."

"It was Sarah. Sarah Winston Beacham."

"Was Winston her maiden name?" Jax asked.

"Yes. I only know that because my wife was talking with her one day, and they found out they both had the same maiden name."

"Thank you again," Jax said. "You've been very helpful. I hope you and your wife have a good evening."

As Jax followed Ace back to the car, he pulled the gold locket from his pocket. He got into the driver's seat. "Guess who gets an extra helping of ice cream when we get home, Ace? I may be way off in left field right now, but there's only one person who comes to my mind with the initials KC." He started the car, and they drove back to the theater.

Jax heard the orchestra as he climbed the stairs. Then, he saw Tim watching the musical offstage in the wings. He couldn't help but laugh. Tim was obviously enjoying himself, smiling and swaying to the music. Then, Jax heard Laura singing, and he quickened his pace to watch her.

Tim leaned over and whispered, "Did you find Beacham?"

Jax pulled his eyes away from the stage and motioned for them to move out of earshot. "He wasn't there. Neither was his copy of the manuscript. But Ace found this under his pillow." He handed Tim the necklace. "It didn't belong to Beacham's wife. Do you want to know what I think?"

"No, but you're going to tell me anyway."

"KC. Kitty Cooper. The men who broke into her house back in March killed her and stole her furs and jewelry, according to the maid. It's in that file you let me borrow. There's also a list of stolen items, everything that the maid could remember. There was a gold locket on that list. It didn't say whether the locket was engraved or not, so we'll need to talk to the maid again."

"If it does belong to Kitty Cooper, then Beacham was involved in her murder. But I thought you said he was an older man? And if his apartment is in our neighborhood, he certainly wasn't living on easy street."

"I know. So, it boils down to this. If that is Kitty's necklace, Beacham killed her or hired a couple of thugs to do the job. And he's responsible for Sanders' death, too. As far as we know, he disappeared with at least his copy of the manuscript."

"Or?" Tim asked.

"Or someone went to a lot of trouble setting Beacham up, and his disappearance wasn't by choice. Either way, Laura isn't going to like this one bit." He quieted when he heard her singing again, and he knew that he could listen to her for hours.

Even Tim was engrossed. "She has a beautiful voice." And they both stood there, quietly.

When the chorus singers took the stage, Jax turned to Tim again. "Laura told me that Beacham had intended to give his copy of the manuscript to the theater director. We need to find out if he has it or not. I think the man's name is Rosenberg, and he's got to be here somewhere."

"I can ask around for him."

"No, I'll do that later. I don't want to distract anyone from the performance. It's late, Murph. Why don't you go home to your family? I'll talk to Rosenberg when it's over, and I'll take Laura home. First thing in the morning, try to find out if there's any connection between Horace Beacham and Robert Ashworth besides being an employee of the theater. If there is, we've got ourselves a handful of suspects. I'll talk to you in the morning."

Tim started walking away, then he turned around. "You know. These musicals are pretty good. No wonder Carla has been bugging me to take her to one."

17
Roommates

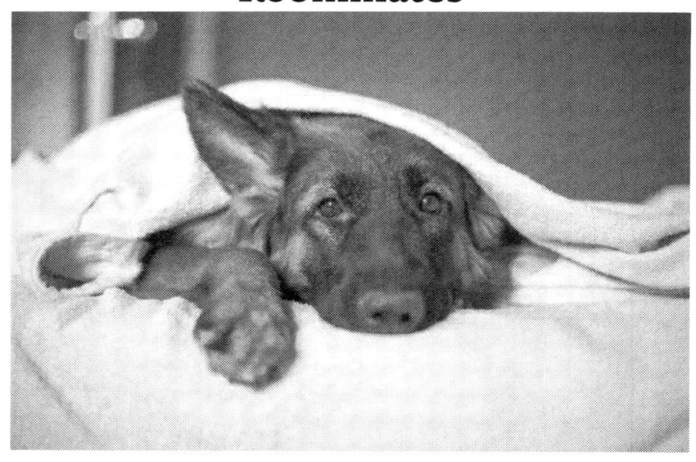

Jax watched the rest of the show from the sidelines, enjoying most of it. Yet, he was also studying those around him who were involved with the production behind the scenes. By the time the performers lined up on stage for the curtain call, he had a pretty good idea who the director might be.

Laura rushed off the stage before the curtain had dropped for the last time. She grabbed Jax's hand and dragged him into her dressing room. Annie was there, and he told them that the manager at the apartment hadn't seen Mister Beacham in the past few days.

"The landlord didn't know where he was?" Laura asked.

"No, I'm sorry." He could tell both women were beside themselves with worry. "Laura, the stage manager said that he spoke with Mister Beacham on Monday. Maybe he did go out of town, and the stage manager misunderstood about him visiting a sister. I looked around his apartment. It was furnished very simply with nothing that seemed out of place." He'd decided not to mention the gold locket right now. There was no point in further upsetting her, at least not until they confirmed who the necklace belonged to. "I'm sure he's fine."

"Isn't there some other way we can find out where he went? He doesn't have a car, so he'd have to travel by train if he went any great distance," Laura told him.

He reached over to hug her, then he pulled fretting Annie into his embrace, too. "We'll find him. As you know, I have a few connections at the police department. I'll make some phone calls. Annie, why don't you help Laura change? I'm going to ask around to see if someone else knows where he may have gone. I won't be long, so wait for me here. Both of you. We'll give you a ride home, Annie."

Jax left the dressing room, and the man he'd pegged as the director was talking with a few of the performers. He stepped closer and overheard their conversation, which confirmed his assumption. After the performers left, Jax introduced himself to the man, and they conversed for a few minutes. When he asked about Mister Beacham, the director told him that he only knew what the stage manager had reported to him. Then, without divulging anything of importance, Jax casually asked about any new manuscripts that he may have received from Horace Beacham lately.

"I haven't seen any, but if Horace has a new script, it's probably in his file cabinet in the music room down the hall."

Jax glanced back at Laura's dressing room. He didn't have time to search for it now, not without mentioning it to Laura. Besides, he figured there was no rush in it anyway. If Beacham didn't take the manuscript with him, it would either still be in the file cabinet in the morning or someone else had already taken it. So, he thanked Mister Rosenberg and made his way back to the dressing room.

They drove to Queens, where Annie lived with her son and his family. Laura sat in the back seat with Ace while Annie talked Jax's ear off about her grandkids. Finally, they dropped her off and headed for Brooklyn.

"Murph and I watched the performance for a while. He had never seen a Broadway play, and he really enjoyed it. I thought you were wonderful. There were several curtain calls, so it went well."

"It did, surprisingly. I'm sorry for sounding so jittery. You have enough to worry about. But Mister Beacham is such a dear man. I'm just so worried about him."

"I understand. Like I said, nothing looked out of the ordinary at his apartment. If he had any type of traveling bag, I didn't find it. So, he probably did take a short holiday."

"I hope you're right."

"Why don't you tell me more about him? How do you know he doesn't have any family?"

"It's very sad." She explained about what he and his wife had gone through in Romania, and how they ended up living here. Then, she talked on about how he had taken her under his wing after she was hired, and that he was so helpful and supportive, even offering to work a few extra hours with her at the theater.

Jax didn't say anything else. She seemed a bit calmer now, but he was still worried. From what she'd said, it didn't sound like Beacham would be involved in any of this. Yet, she'd only had a business relationship with the man and didn't know him personally. Any stories that he had told her about his past, could be just that. Stories. Although, the apartment manager had seemed to like the man, too, and hadn't seen anything unusual going on there.

Still, Beacham had worked for the Ashworths at the theater, and he kept the gold locket under his pillow as though it had sentimental value to him. So, he wasn't about to dismiss the man's guilt.

After Jax parked the car, he walked Laura up to her apartment. "I want you to get a good night's sleep. I'll make a few calls first thing in the morning and let you know if I find out anything."

"I appreciate it, Jax," she said as they walked down the hallway. She pulled out her apartment key, but he smiled at her and took the key to open the door for her.

Just as he lifted his hand to insert the key into the doorknob, he stopped. The door was ajar. With his other arm, he gently moved Laura behind him. "Wait here." And he pushed the door open.

Laura gasped when they saw the apartment had been ransacked, and Jax cursed under his breath. Cautiously, he took a few steps inside. He scanned the kitchen and living areas and checked behind the door. Every cupboard and drawer had been left open with their entire contents, boxes, and cans of food, and silverware dumped on the floor. Even the icebox had been emptied. In the living room, chairs and tables were overturned, cushions tossed about, and the vase that held the flowers he'd given her was smashed with only remnants of the petals strewed about.

Laura was stunned as she came up behind him. He quickly turned around and held her by the shoulders. "Please, Laura, stay in the hall. I want to make sure whoever did this is gone."

She covered her mouth to stifle her tears, and she backed away. Jax slowly walked through the destruction to her bedroom, and it looked like a cyclone had hit the entire place. Her dresser drawers were left open and empty with clothes thrown about. So, too, was her closet. And the mattress of her bed had been flipped over. When he was sure no one else was in the apartment, he made his way back to her.

She stood there, struggling not to cry, and he pulled her into his arms. "Where is the manuscript that Sam Sanders gave you?"

"I have it in my handbag."

He wiped the tears from her eyes and brushed a few curls from her face to look at her. "The place is a mess, but I want you to grab a few things. You're going to stay with me and Ace, tonight."

She nodded.

"We'll come back tomorrow to clean it up, okay. Just take what you need for the night. I'll come with you."

He kept her close to him with his arm around her as they

walked into the bedroom. She remained quiet as she knelt on the floor and began picking through the clutter. She stuffed a few things into her handbag, and Jax walked her out. He locked the door, and they made their way to his car.

They drove in silence to his apartment. Inside, he left her and Ace on the couch while he went into his bedroom and set her handbag down. Then, he grabbed two bottles of beer from the icebox. When he entered the living room, Ace had laid his head in her lap, and she was petting him. He handed her the bottle and sat on the other side of her.

"Who would do that, Jax?" she asked softly.

"Let's not talk about it now. You're safe here."

"Why did you ask about my copy of the manuscript? Is that what they were looking for?"

He fell silent.

Laura suddenly leaned forward, firmly set the bottle of beer down on the table, and stood up, startling both Jax and Ace. "I know I'm upset. I have every right to be between Mister Beacham, and now, my apartment. But I am not a child," she said as she swallowed hard to stop herself from crying. "There's something you aren't telling me, isn't there? You're always making some wisecrack to lighten the mood, especially in a precarious situation. You haven't done that once tonight. So, I know you're keeping something from me. Like when you didn't tell me that we were being followed at the amusement park. But I'm directly involved now, Jax, so I need you to tell me. Please."

He watched her. "You're right. I didn't realize how well you're getting to know me. Last week, I was more honest and open with you about the case than I was with Murph. But things are different now. I care about you, Laura, and I guess because of that, and the fact that you are directly involved, I've lost my sense of humor."

She stood there for a moment. Then, she sat down beside him and smiled. "Well, it's too out of character for you, Detective Diamond. As corny as they are, I prefer hearing your wisecracks when things get tense. And don't let a few of my tears throw you off. I'm stronger than you think."

He lifted her hand and held a kiss upon it. "Oh, I know you are, Miss Graystone. And I will tell you everything that happened today but in the morning. There isn't anything that either of us can do about it right now since it's nearly one o'clock. I'll make us a nice breakfast, and we'll have a long talk to figure out what we do next. I promise."

She wrapped her arms around him and hugged him. "Thank you. Now, who gets the bed?"

"You do, of course. I have extra blankets and pillows in the cupboard. Ace and I will be just fine and dandy sleeping out here on this small, hard sofa."

She quickly kissed his cheek. "Good night, Jax." As she headed into the bedroom, Ace leaped down and followed her. He glanced back at Jax for a second, then slipped inside the room just before Laura closed the door.

"Find friend you are, Ace," Jax grumbled.

18
The Missing Ring

Thursday, June 7

"You're wrong about Mister Beacham, Jax," Laura insisted as they sat at the table the next morning, eating scrambled eggs and buttered toast. Jax had explained everything to her, right down to Kitty Cooper's gold locket. "It's difficult enough thinking that Robert Ashworth is capable of killing someone, possibly two people, but I know Mister Beacham had absolutely nothing to do with this."

"I'm struggling with that, too, but we've got evidence that points to his guilt. At least I think we do. Tim's going to talk with Kitty Cooper's maid and see if she can confirm the necklace belonged to Kitty."

"Well, I think that finding Mister Beacham takes precedence over everything else."

"I told you. Murph has a few men working on it. They'll let us know as soon as they find out anything. The first thing I want to do is go to the theater to see if Mister Beacham's copy of the manuscript is in his file cabinet. Since you don't have a performance tonight, I was wondering if the back door to the theater would be open?"

"The maintenance crew is usually there by eight o'clock. I'm going with you."

He nearly choked on his coffee. "Over my dead body! I'm not putting you in any more danger. Whoever broke into your apartment last night was looking for the manuscript, and they didn't find it. So, their next step is forcing you to tell them where it is. That's why you're staying put right here with Ace. One of Murph's officers is already on his way over to keep an eye on you, too."

She shrugged her shoulders. "I am not staying here like some prisoner. Besides, you don't have any legal right to be in the theater without a search warrant. So, they'll just boot you out of there. You need me to get you inside."

He opened his mouth to object, but he knew she was right and let out a defeated sigh instead.

"I also want to go to my apartment sometime today to straighten up and pack a few more things. I agree that I shouldn't stay there right now, but I'm going to talk to Jeanie and Margie. I know they won't have any objections to letting me stay with them for a while. I'm very grateful to you, Jax, but I feel bad putting you out like this. It couldn't have been comfortable sleeping on that sofa."

"I'm stomping my foot on that idea," he told her. "If you stay with your friends, then you're putting them in danger, too, whether you tell them what's going on or not. At least here, you're safe since you have both me and Ace." She fell silent. "And we're giving your copy of the manuscript to Murph to keep at the station. I don't want to lose that copy. If push comes to shove, we'll use it as bait to catch Robert Ashworth or whoever is behind this in the act."

"Jax, remember when you explained to me that a motive was needed to convict a criminal? You mentioned before that Patricia Sanders was having trouble getting a divorce, so that would be her motive for her husband's death, right? But after you overheard the conversation yesterday at the Ashworth's mansion, it seems that Robert had two motives for killing Samuel Sanders. Being with his wife and retaining the rights to his manuscript."

"That's why Ashworth is still my top suspect."

She nodded. "We also know that Robert and Kitty Cooper were having a secret affair. Jeanie is the one who told me that she'd heard rumors about it, but Margie said she saw the two of them at that cafe on Fulton Street sometime over the winter. They were arguing and Kitty stormed out. So, he possibly has a motive for killing Kitty Cooper, too. But now, you think Mister Beacham was involved in her death? What would be his motive?"

"I can't answer that yet. All I know is that I found that gold necklace in his apartment, and if it did belong to Kitty, he's involved with all of this, somehow."

"Okay, take Mister Beacham out of it for a minute since I don't believe he's involved," she went on thoughtfully. "I think we're both sure that neither Patricia Sanders nor Robert Ashworth would risk murdering anyone on their own. With their wealth, they would hire other people to take care of the task for them. How did Kitty Cooper die?"

"An overdose of chloroform after some thugs broke into her apartment," he told her. "And they deliberately made it look like a robbery to throw the police off their trail. The same men might have broken into your apartment last night, which is why..."

"Yet, in Mister Sanders' case, he was killed by eating some poisonous plant. I don't know, Jax. If Robert Ashworth hired those men to kill Kitty Cooper, why not pay them to kill Mister Sanders in the same manner? Especially since those men got away with it. It doesn't seem to me that the two murders are related."

"Except that in both cases, we found a white lily in their possession."

"Even so, the horrible way poor Mister Sanders died was very different than the way Kitty was killed. Doesn't his death seem far more calculating and personal?"

"Good point," he muttered.

She stood up and started collecting their plates. "If I'm going to stay here, I insist on washing the dishes. I can't cook, so it's the least I can do. Then, we'll take our little trip to the theater."

Jax groaned. "I'm too tired to argue with you."

"We're also going to have to come up with a believable story to tell Jeanie and Margie. Jeanie especially will notice right off that I'm not at my apartment or answering the phone. Nothing slips by her. And I don't want either of them knowing that I'm staying with you. They will both take *that* way out of context."

"We'll think of something."

She placed the dishes in the sink, and her mind was spinning in every direction. "You know. I can't stop thinking about Missus Ashworth. If her son is involved in this, I can't imagine how she'll react. She both coddles and ridicules Robert, but he's her only son. This could destroy her."

"It's not like she's completely innocent, Laura," Jax told her. "She paid someone a lot of money to quash the investigation against her son in the Kitty Cooper case, and she managed to keep his name out the newspapers."

Within the hour, they entered the back door of the Ambassador. Immediately, they were met by a few of the maintenance crew who recognized Laura and greeted them. She led the way upstairs towards her dressing room, but instead, they continued down the hallway to the music room. Jax made sure no one else was around before opening the door, then they slipped inside and found Mister Beacham's file cabinet against the far wall.

"Which drawer do you want to look in?" Jax asked.

"There are only two drawers, Jax. Pick one."

He chose the bottom drawer, pulled it out, and sifted through it. Yet, between the two of them, it wasn't long before they were both disappointed that they didn't find anything. "I had a feeling it wouldn't be here."

"Now what?" she asked.

"I have another idea that you're not going to like very much. I'm assuming Robert Ashworth has an office somewhere here in the theater. I didn't see his car out front, so I thought that we could take a quick peek." He watched her hazel eyes grow wide and aghast, and he started laughing. "Hey, you insisted on coming here with me today. Think of it as another fun adventure."

She shook her head, heaved an irritated sigh, and headed for the door. "His office is upstairs. If we're caught, I'm going to be fired."

Rather than sneak around like thieves, Laura and Jax boldly walked across the stage to the left side of the theater as though they had a justifiable purpose. Silently, they climbed the wooden stairway to the second floor. Laura stopped at the top to make sure the coast was clear, then she led Jax to the second door at the end of the small hallway.

She turned around and folded her arms. "I'll stay out here and knock on the door if I hear someone coming. I feel guilty enough doing this. I don't want to go in there."

"Okay, you be the lookout," he chuckled, and he pulled out his pocketknife.

"You're going to break in?"

"I'm sure Ashworth keeps it locked."

She reached over, turned the knob and the door swung open.

"Huh."

"Just hurry up," she snapped at him.

Jax glanced around the room. To be truthful, he didn't like being here any more than she did. Even if he found something, he couldn't legally remove it without getting into a whole lot of trouble himself. Still, he was too curious to go back now. Inside the room, there was an oak rolltop desk and chair, a small meeting table with three more wooden chairs, and a single drawer file cabinet.

As quickly as he could, he searched the file cabinet first. Each folder inside was neatly labeled and either stuffed with financial reports or expense receipts. If he'd had more time, he would have loved to look more closely at the financials, but right now, they were irrelevant. When he was satisfied that it didn't hold a copy of the manuscript, he shifted his attention to the rolltop desk. He began opening the larger drawers. Yet, they were all empty except for one that merely contained a few office utensils.

Jax shoved the rolltop open next. He found a ledger and flipped through it, but it dealt with employee hours and payroll.

He focused on the cubbies and small drawers along the inside of the desk. There were several unopened envelopes stacked in the slots on the top right side, and they were all company-related bills and such. He opened the first of two small drawers on the upper left side, and he knew right off he'd hit the jackpot.

There was a man's gold ring inside. He yanked the drawer out, grabbed the handkerchief from his pocket, and used it to look at the ring. It was solid gold with a pattern of etchings and an inlay of seven tiny diamonds. When he turned it around, he saw the engraving, SMS.

Laura tapped on the door, startling him. He quickly replaced the ring, shoved the drawer back into the slot, and joined her in the hallway. She whispered that a few of the maintenance crew had begun cleaning the floors just below them.

"Follow me," she said, and she opened the first door they had passed which led to a back stairway.

"I never realized how big these theaters were," he told her as they hurried down the steps.

"You haven't seen the half of it. On the other side of the crossover, there's another office and stairway just like this, plus several hidden catwalks. Below the stage, there are at least a dozen storage rooms on the lower level, along with the trap room. And even more storage and equipment rooms in the basement, which is where these stairs end up. But there is also a street exit down there that leads to the back alley. So, did you find anything in his office?"

"A gold mine, literally. I'll tell you about it once you find our way out of here."

At the bottom of the stairwell, she pushed the door open to the basement, and they rushed through the room to a hallway. "A few stairwells lead to the basement, but the only other exit is at the opposite end of the theater. After I was hired, Mister Kratz showed me around the entire theater. When he brought me down here, and we started going through this maze of corridors, I told him that I would get lost and never find my out."

But the hallway ended. "Which way?" Jax asked.

"We take a right. I'll get us out of here," Laura assured him as they hurried down another hallway. "Each hallway splits in both directions at the end, so it's very confusing. Mister Kratz explained that there was a little trick to finding your way through. At the end of the first hallway, turning left leads to a storage room, and turning right leads you down another hallway. Then, you need to reverse it. The next right turn takes you to another room, a left turn takes you down a hallway. So, it's a right, left, right kind of pattern."

"Feels like a jumbled-up mess to me," Jax muttered. "I hope you're keeping track."

Laura kept leading the way through several more hallways until they finally reached the stairwell. "See? It worked."

Jax opened the door to the alley and they headed back to his car. "We're going to the precinct now. I need Murph to get a court order right away to search that office legally, and before Ashworth gets wind of it."

"What did you find?" she asked.

"Sam Sanders' gold ring." And he couldn't be more thrilled to finally have some substantial evidence against Robert Ashworth. "I knew Sanders was wearing a ring the night he was killed. There was an indent of one on his middle finger, but I couldn't find it in the apartment. Patricia Sanders confirmed that he always wore a gold ring."

"How can you be sure it's Mister Sanders' ring?"

Jax started laughing. "You'd think crooks would be smart enough not to steal anything that has the victim's initials on it."

19
The Lily Pond

It was shortly after ten-thirty when Jax escorted Laura into the station house with Ace following behind them. As they walked down one of the aisles with desks on either side, some officers greeted them, others hooted softly, and a few whistled at Laura after they passed.

"Careful, boys!" Jax announced loudly as they went. "Ace will rip your arm off if you treat her with disrespect."

Laura stifled a giggle when all the officers fell silent and sat down.

They found Tim at his desk. Jax explained how he happened upon the ring, and Tim furiously started lecturing him about forced entries and illegal searches, but Jax cut him off. "I didn't take the ring, Murph. It's still in his rolltop desk. You need to get a search warrant right away, and make sure no one alerts Robert Ashworth, or that ring will disappear before you get there."

Tim settled down and agreed with him. "Let me talk with Lieutenant Simmons about it. Maybe we can skirt around Captain Ryan for now since he seems sympathetic with the Ashworths. Once we have it in our possession, we'll report everything to him. We found the woman who was Kitty Cooper's maid. I just finished talking with her. She said that Kitty's initials were definitely on the gold locket."

"Did you find out where Mister Beacham is?" Laura asked anxiously.

"So far, his name hasn't been on any railroad ticket rosters that we've seen. But we have no idea when he left town, except it was probably between last Thursday and Monday morning. It'll take a while to check all the departures."

"Thank you, Tim. Here is my copy of the manuscript," she said as she pulled it from her handbag. "Jax said it would be safer in your hands than ours."

"I agree with him," Tim replied.

"We're going back to Laura's apartment now, Murph. It'll take us a while to clean up the mess, so give me a call there as soon as you get that warrant."

"Be careful and stay out of trouble. Both of you," Tim added.

Jax brought Ace upstairs with them after they arrived at Laura's apartment. Laura grew emotional again when she saw the destruction inside. Yet, she forced herself to concentrate on getting everything back in order. She started sweeping up the broken plates and glasses in the kitchen while Jax went into the living room to straighten the overturned furniture and replace the cushions.

They weren't there more than ten minutes when someone knocked on the door. Jax told Laura to stay in the kitchen while he answered it with Ace by his side. He only opened the door a crack and recognized Jeanie.

"Well, hello again," she greeted with a smile.

"Nice to see you, Jeanie."

"Laura hasn't answered her phone. Now I know why," she snickered as she struggled to peek inside the apartment.

"She's busy in the kitchen right now. Can I have her..."

"I won't stay but a minute." She pushed on the door, so Jax finally opened it. Jeanie's hands flew over her mouth when she gasped. "Oh, no! What happened? Laura!" She swept by Jax, but just before reaching the kitchen, she yelped again and froze seeing Ace standing there. "Does he bite?"

"Only when I tell him to," Jax kidded as he came up behind her.

"Don't listen to him, Jeanie. Ace is a sweetheart," Laura laughed. And she explained that someone had broken into her apartment last night when she wasn't home.

"How wretched! No place is safe in the city anymore. This is awful, Laura. Why on earth would someone do this? You can't possibly stay here. Not until those horrible scoundrels are caught. Let me fetch Margie, and we'll both help you clean up. We'll pack a few of your belongings, and you can stay with us for a few days. It'll be fun. Like those sleepovers we used to have when we were kids."

Laura stared at Jax, not knowing what to say.

"We've already settled it, Jeanie," he told her. "Laura is staying with my younger sister, Lucinda. She has a nice apartment not far from here with a spare bedroom." He shrugged his shoulders at Laura while Jeanie's head swiveled back and forth between them. "Lucinda is more than happy to help out."

"Oh. That's nice, I guess," Jeanie said. "But Margie and I will still help you clean up. I'll fetch her and be back in a flash." And she scooted out the door.

Laura let out the breath she was holding. "That was quick thinking, Jax. Do you really have a sister named Lucinda?"

"Sure do, let's see. I think she's the second youngest girl in our family."

"I still find it amazing that you have eleven siblings. Do any of them live in the city?"

"No, they're all homebodies. Some still live with my parents upstate and the others are scattered around close to them." And he headed back into the living room.

"If I know Jeanie, she'll ask for your sister's telephone number and address."

"I'll give her mine," he said. "That's the best I could up with under pressure. Besides, if she does stop by, she won't be surprised to see me there, too."

"Well, it's better than telling her the truth," Laura laughed.

When Jeanie returned, she said that Margie had just gotten out of bed. "She didn't get home until the wee hours of the morning. She told me that practice ran late at the theater last night, but I think she had a date that she's keeping under wraps. Has she said anything to you, Laura? She's gone more than she's home lately."

Laura felt bad lying to her again. "No, not a word."

"She offered to help after she got dressed, but then I told her about *him.*" Jeanie pointed at Ace. "She's allergic to dogs. Who knew?"

For the next few hours, the three of them worked diligently to clean up each room. Then, Jeanie and Laura went back into the bedroom to pack some of her clothes. Jax was waiting for them in the living room when the telephone rang, and he quickly answered it. But as he listened to what Tim had to say, he slowly turned around towards the bedroom door. Laura was standing there, so he kept his responses short. When he finally hung up, he remained silent for a moment, not knowing how to tell her.

"That was Tim on the phone, wasn't it?" she asked.

"Yeah. He got the search warrant, and his men are at the theater right now."

"What else did he say, Jax? I can tell by the look on your face that something is wrong."

He hesitated again. "We need to take a ride to Fort Greene Park."

"The Park?"

He saw the fear in her eyes and felt it, himself. "The police found something there." She didn't respond, so he went over to her. "We need to leave. Tell Jeanie that we're done here for now, and you'll call her later."

She nodded and disappeared into the bedroom. Within seconds, the two of them emerged. Jeanie kept talking to Laura about something trivial while she carried her leather bag and hangers with dresses, skirts, and blouses. She forced a smile and kept nodding to her friend. Jax took the bag and clothes from her, cut Jeanie off by explaining that his sister was waiting for them, and they finally left the building.

The short drive to the park was quiet and painful for both of them. Without saying a word, Jax knew Laura was well aware that this had to do with Horace Beacham, but he just couldn't bring himself to say it aloud. And he dreaded the moment she saw for herself.

He parked the car along the side of the road. There were several police cars lined up across the street directly in front of the park, along with a Model-T ambulance. Jax got out of the car and went around to open the door for her, but he bent down and took a deep breath. "They found a body in the pond, Laura."

She was trembling, and her voice quivered as she spoke. "It's Mister Beacham, isn't it?"

"Murph said they're pretty sure, but they need someone to identify him. If you don't want to do this, I'll take you to my apartment right now, and call someone else at the theater or the manager at his apartment."

"No, I don't want anyone else to see him this way."

"And I don't want you to. I hate putting you through this."

She sat there. "Jax, I think this would be the perfect time for one of your wisecracks."

"I wish I could think of one, Laura."

She got out of the car and clung to him as they walked into the park. There was a crowd of people by the pond. As they grew closer, several police officers were grouped together. Tim saw them and broke away from the others.

"I am sorry, Laura," he told her.

When she saw the covered body on the ground, her knees nearly gave way, but Jax tightened his grip, and Ace leaned against her leg on the other side. Then, she looked up at Jax with tears in her eyes.

"The coroner isn't sure how long he's been in the water with the pond temperature being so cool this time of year," he said quietly. "Still, he won't look the same as you remember him. They just need you to take a quick peek at him, enough to identify him. I'll tell you now, it's going to be an image that will stick with you for a long time. So please, Laura, make sure you're up to doing this. There is nothing cowardly about walking away right now."

"Just stay with me, both of you," she said, glancing at Ace.

"We're not going anywhere," Jax assured her.

They walked forward. Murph pulled the sheet down, just far enough to uncover his face, then he covered it back up again.

Tears streamed down Laura's cheeks now as she nodded. "Yes, it's Mister Beacham."

Tim stood up. He told the coroner's men to take the body to the ambulance that awaited, and he approached them. "I'll let you know what we find at the theater. If that ring is still there, Lieutenant Simmons said that he would speak with Captain Ryan and insist upon arresting Robert Ashworth." After Jax thanked him, Tim turned to Laura. "Do you want me to ask Carla to stop by? She's very supportive in situations like this."

"No, Tim. That's very kind of you, but please don't trouble her. I'm all right. I knew something bad had happened to him. Not this, but close to it. I appreciate everything you've done."

"Well, if there's anything else you need, you know where to find me. I'll stay in touch with both of you."

Jax and Ace walked her back to the car.

"This is so sad," she said as they drove to the apartment. "Mister Beacham was such a sweet man. He and his wife had lived through so much heartache. Horrors that we cannot even imagine. And without any other family, it's as though he never existed."

"You'll never forget him, Laura, and I'm sure there are others at the theater who feel the same. Even the manager of his apartment and his wife thought very highly of him."

She fell silent as a thought struck her. She leaned forward, gripped the dashboard, and turned to Jax. "When we were at Tim's house, you said that you found a white lily at Kitty Cooper's and another one in Mister Sanders' apartment, connecting the two murders. The pond was full of water lilies, Jax."

"I know."

"Robert Ashworth did this, didn't he?" she cried. "All for that stupid manuscript. I don't care how much it's worth. I hope you put him in jail for the rest of his life!"

"We will, Laura, trust me." He knew her thoughts and emotions were bouncing all over the place right now, and it would take time before they started settling down.

"The pond," she blurted out in panic. "Oh, Jax, we walked around that pond last Sunday before we went on the ferry."

"Laura, please don't do this to yourself."

Her breaths were coming quick as she gripped the dashboard tighter. "But Mister Beacham could have been in the pond while we were strolling around. What if he was still alive? We could have..."

Ace suddenly darted forward and started licking her hair and face. Instantly, he distracted her, and she began to calm down. She hugged him tightly and whispered her thanks. And Jax thanked him, too.

20
An Arrest

Jax hated to leave Laura at the apartment, but Tim had called, and he didn't want to miss the satisfaction of watching them arrest Robert Ashworth. Thankfully, Laura had laid down on the bed to rest, and Ace was with her. And Murph was sending over two police officers to stand guard by his front door and keep an eye on things while he was gone.

According to Tim, they had found Sam Sanders' ring in the desk at the theater, and Captain Ryan had not only been informed of the events, but he insisted upon making the arrest himself. So, Jax drove to Fifth Avenue, parked his car, and nearly laughed out loud seeing all the hullabaloo. He knew then that the captain had regretted allowing Ashworth to walk away unscathed after Kitty Cooper's murder. Otherwise, there wouldn't be so much fanfare right now.

While the ring may have been proof enough to convict Ashworth but finding Horace Beacham murdered guaranteed it. Obviously, Ashworth had the gold locket placed at Beacham's apartment in a feeble attempt to trick the police.

In his mind, Patricia Sanders was off the hook. When he questioned the woman at her apartment before the funeral, she spoke freely about her husband's ring and adamantly requested that it be returned to her. If she had been an accomplice and knew that her lover had the ring in his possession, she wouldn't even have mentioned it. Outside of that, it didn't seem she had anything to do with Kitty Cooper, except she started seeing Robert Ashworth after the woman's death.

Jax jumped out of the car when he saw the officers escorting the furious, hand-cuffed millionaire down the front steps. He hurried across the street to get a closer view and leaned against the police car that was parked out front to haul the man to the station.

"Carlton!" Robert shouted. "Tell my lawyer to meet me at the thirteenth precinct! I swear you are going to pay for this Captain Ryan!"

Jax smiled at him. "You're all washed up, Ashworth. Let's see your mother get you out of this one. Or two."

"Go to hell, Diamond!"

"Right behind you, Ashworth."

Tim stood beside him, chuckling. "That's hitting him below the belt, Jax." They watched Robert get into the backseat, and the car drove off. "How is Laura holding up?"

"She'll be okay, especially now with Ashworth behind bars."

"Ralph Boyer is looking through those financial records you found in Ashworth's office at the theater, and some of our men are inside the mansion, searching every room for a copy of the manuscript. Hopefully, they find something that leads us to the men who Ashworth had hired to do his dirty work. Then Laura will be safe, and she can move back into her own apartment."

"I kind of like having her around. So does Ace."

"Missus Ashworth is still at their summer home. Captain Ryan is trying to contact her."

"Won't she be surprised?" Jax laughed. "When will you be questioning him? I'd like to be close by."

"Not until tomorrow morning. He's going to be a hard egg to crack."

"If you hit him in the right spot, he'll shatter. Especially since he doesn't have a leg to stand on. I'll see you in the morning, Murph."

On his way home, Jax stopped at the local delicatessen. He picked up a few cans of chicken soup and a loaf of Italian bread. He assumed Laura wouldn't have much of an appetite just yet. If she did, he could call his favorite Chinese joint around the corner and pay them to deliver it.

Jax thanked the officers who were still in the hallway guarding his apartment, and he found Laura and Ace on the sofa together. Ace was practically laying in her lap, and Jax got a real kick out of how quickly he'd become attached to her. Ace didn't even lift his head when he walked into the room.

"Robert Ashworth is in custody now," he said as he sat down beside them. "And it won't take long to find whoever else was involved."

"I'm glad," she said quietly.

"I have plenty of chicken noodle soup, or I can order Chinese. I wasn't sure how hungry you'd be."

"Soup is fine. Thank you."

He stretched his arm over Ace and rested his hand on her shoulder. "What can I do for you, Laura?"

"You've done so much already. I truly appreciate it. I learned the hard way a long time ago that when you lose someone you care about, as sad and heartbreaking as it is, you can't go back and change what happened. I should arrange some sort of funeral for him. Someone has to. I don't want his life to be erased so quickly."

"Joe Marsh, the coroner, is a friend of mine with a big heart. I think he would be more than willing to put a funeral together at little or no cost."

"That would make me feel so better, Jax. There won't be many people. Just a simple gathering would be nice."

"I'll give him a call."

She smiled at him. "Did you say Chinese? A couple of rice rolls and some chop suey sounds delicious right now."

He laughed. "Consider it done.

The next morning, Jax heard the bathroom door open. His

legs were draped uncomfortably over the other side of the sofa, and his blanket lay in a crumpled pile on the floor with his pillow buried underneath somewhere. His neck ached and his back was killing him from sleeping in a crunched and crooked position all night. And when he sat up, he groaned in pain.

"Good morning, Jax," Laura greeted cheerfully. "I hope you don't mind, but I took a nice, hot bath and stole one of your dress shirts. I forgot to bring my robe with me." She was towel-drying her hair, and his white striped shirt barely covered her knees.

"What's mine is yours, I guess," he muttered as he rubbed his neck.

She sat down in the chair beside him. "What's for breakfast? Ace and I are starving. It's nearly nine-thirty already."

"Nine-thirty?" He bolted to his feet. "I have to get down to the station. They're questioning Robert Ashworth this morning."

"Oh, I'm sorry. I wish you had told me." She reached over to pet Ace. "I didn't think I would sleep very well, but knowing Robert Ashworth is in custody helped. I called Mister Kratz at the theater earlier. The director had already told him what had happened to Mister Beacham, and he felt as badly as I do about it. He didn't mention knowing about Robert Ashworth's arrest, so I didn't say anything. As far as he knew, we still have a performance tonight. It will be tough for everyone. I called Annie, too, and let her know. She was heartbroken. Could we stop by to talk to your coroner friend about a funeral before we go to the station? If he's willing, I can let everyone at the theater know about it at our rehearsal later this afternoon."

Jax was staring at her, and her scant appearance. He shook his head to get rid of his indecent thoughts. "I'll give Joe a call before I leave and ask him. I want you and Ace to stay here in the apartment while I'm gone. There are plenty of corn muffins in the cupboard. You didn't happen to make any coffee, did you?"

"The cups are on the counter and the kettle is full. It'll only take a minute. But Jax, I don't want to stay here all day. Can't we come with you?"

He looked at the pleading expression on her face, then his eyes wandered to her legs again. He stood up. "Okay, I'll heat the kettle while you get dressed."

When they arrived at the police station, Tim wasn't at his desk, so Jax led Laura around the corner to the back rooms where they interviewed criminals, victims, and witnesses. A few officers were standing around drinking coffee in the hall, including Tim.

"Are they questioning Robert Ashworth now?" Jax asked.

"Captain Ryan, Lieutenant Simmons, and a few other officials, including the commissioner are in there with him now. His lawyer showed up, too. Ralph Boyer finished reviewing those financial records and wrote a lengthy, detailed report on them. If we can't pin any of the murders on Robert Ashworth, we sure as heck have a solid case against him for bootlegging and money laundering stemming from his close business relationship with Orin Marino."

"What a surprise. I gather Ashworth hasn't confessed to the murders yet?"

"He's putting up quite a fight. He keeps denying having anything to do with Sanders' death. He also said that he doesn't know anything about the ring, or how it got into his desk. He's even claiming that there was nothing personal going on between him and Kitty Cooper."

"We know that's a lie," Laura spouted, gathering their attention. "Well, we do!"

"When they asked about Horace Beacham's death," Tim continued. "He acted surprised as though he knew nothing about it."

"Your men didn't happen to come across a couple of copies of Sanders' manuscript at the mansion, did they?"

"Nope. No manuscripts or poisonous plants." Tim held up his index finger. "But wait, there's more. Orin Marino is waiting impatiently in the second interview room. Those financial records are as damaging to him as they are Robert Ashworth, so he's got a lot of explaining to do. Two of Marino's thugs who had received payments directly from Robert Ashworth are in the third room. And Patricia Sanders is pacing back and forth like a caged tiger in the fourth room. We're not sure if she had anything to do with this, or whether she knows anything of importance. But she gave the officers such a tough time at her apartment when they showed her the search warrant, they brought her in just to shut her up."

Jax laughed. "You have a full house."

Laura suddenly slipped behind Jax, whispering, "Missus Ashworth is here."

Both Jax and Tim turned around. The woman was heading their way with her thick-heeled black oxford shoes pounding the floor as furiously as the contorted scowl on her face. They all backed away against the far wall to let her pass. Laura tried to remain hidden behind Jax, but the woman spotted her and halted directly in front of them.

"Laura!" Missus Ashworth barked.

She slowly came forward despite Jax's subtle effort to stop her. "Yes, Missus Ashworth."

"What are you doing here? Where is my son!" the woman demanded.

Laura pointed to the first room. "He's inside with his lawyer, ma'am."

Missus Ashworth flashed her a disapproving glare and headed for the door. Tim stepped forward. "I'm sorry, Missus Ashworth. You need to wait until..." But the woman stormed inside the room and slammed the door behind her.

"Well, so much for your authority," Jax kidded.

"I'm used to it being friends with you."

"Can I use your phone, Murph?" he asked. "I told Laura that I'd call Joe Marsh to see if he could arrange a small funeral for Horace Beacham, and I forgot."

"Help yourself. You know where it is."

Jax headed off. "I'll be right back. Don't talk about me while I'm gone!"

Tim laughed as he watched him walk away. "He's a real character, isn't he?"

Laura smiled, too. "Yes, he is. He told me last weekend that he kind of grows on people. He's right. Have you met the rest of his family? I wondered if they were all just as clever and goofy as he is. With such a big family, he's probably not the only one."

Tim lost his mirth and checked the office area to make sure Jax was out of sight. "He doesn't have any family, Laura."

She looked at him queerly, thinking he was joking. Then, she saw the pained expression on his face. "But Jax has talked about his family, Tim. He said that he grew up in the country in upstate New York. He's mentioned his parents and his mother. And he has a younger sister named Lucinda. Why would he say all that if it wasn't true?"

"He made up those stories to avoid talking about his childhood with anyone. That's what he told me. But I think it's his way of coping with the truth, and probably wishful thinking on his part." She looked up at him, and he took a deep breath. "Someone left him on the doorstep of an orphan asylum when he was a newborn. He never told me which one. There wasn't a note in the basket or anything to let them know what his name was or where he was from. Just one single playing card tucked underneath him, the jack of diamonds. The nun who found him there decided to name him, Jax Diamond."

She wandered a few steps away from him, thinking about it.

"He didn't tell me about it for quite some time, even though we quickly became good friends on top of being partners. But after several holidays went by, I realized that he never visited his family, and no one visited him, so I confronted him about it. He finally told me the truth and confessed that it was one of the reasons he became a police officer. He'd hoped to have better access in tracking his mother down. He said he didn't care what her reasons were for giving him up. He just wanted to know why she didn't leave any sort of clue as to who he was. But so far, he hasn't had any luck."

Laura felt horrible for Jax. She didn't even want to think about what her life would have been like without her family.

She'd had such a wonderful childhood, safe, tight-knit, and loving. And after her father died, his death merely brought her, her mother, and brother even closer together.

"From what I gather, Jax had it pretty rough inside that orphanage," Tim went on. "He ran away several times, but the police or some concerned citizen kept dragging him back there. He wasn't allowed to leave until he turned sixteen. That's a lot of years in a kid's life. Please, Laura, don't say anything to him. I don't want him to know that I told you about it."

She turned around to face him again. "Of course, I won't."

"Jax irritates the heck out of me. But I love him like a brother."

"He feels the same about you, it's easy to see. He's lucky to have you as a friend, Tim, and I'm glad you confided in me. Did he leave the police force to search for his family on his own?"

"No, that's a whole other sad story in his life and something else that's been eating at him. I think I've said enough. Here he comes."

21
The Gardenias

Still Friday, June 8

Laura and Jax stayed at the station until Lieutenant Simmons emerged from the room, looking as though he'd been through the mill. He had a few choice words about Missus Ashworth, then he told them that they were keeping Robert Ashworth locked up pending a determination of bail. Laura had no desire to face Missus Ashworth again, so she and Jax left to meet with Joe Marsh regarding the funeral.

By mid-afternoon, they were heading for the theater since Laura didn't want to miss the rehearsal. But she couldn't stop thinking about what Tim had told her. Discreetly, she glanced over Jax.

What had happened to him was tragic. So, too, was his earnest effort to cover it all up. That in itself was proof whatever he went through as a child must have been wretched. Yet, knowing the truth made better sense of his jovial attitude, scoffing off danger, and clowning around. Like a defense to cover up the pain inside of him.

"Joe Marsh seems very nice," she said, pulling herself back into the moment. "Thank you for stopping by his office and asking him to do this, Jax. I'm so glad that I can pay tribute to Mister Beacham this way. Having it on Monday morning will give everyone fair notice. And Greenwood Cemetery sounds beautiful and with such rich history."

"Murph said that he and some of the officers want to attend the funeral, so we'll need to let him know. Everyone feels lousy about what happened to him. By rights, the Ashworths should pay for the whole thing."

"I have a little money saved that I'd like to give to Mister Marsh."

"Joe won't accept it from you, but he'd charge them triple."

At the theater, they entered through the back door. Laura grew worried as they made their way upstairs. It was eerily quiet. Not a soul passed them on the stairwell, and the hallway on the second floor was empty, except for Mister Kratz who was standing offstage talking with a few of the stage crew.

When he saw them, he finished giving the other men their instructions and walked over. He said that the director had postponed all performances indefinitely, and he was sending everyone home. Laura wasn't too surprised, but she was disappointed. She told him about the funeral arrangements, and he very kindly agreed to handle notifying the theater employees.

"Not everyone has a telephone, but I'll call those who do," he assured her. "I didn't think Horace had any living relatives, so I'm grateful to you for organizing it. He was one of the nicest men I've ever known."

"I thought the world of him, too, Mister Kratz." She turned to Jax. "It'll just take me a minute to gather a few things before we leave."

"Laura, there was a delivery for you about an hour ago," Mister Kratz told her. "Jimmy signed for it and put it in your dressing room."

"That's odd. I wasn't expecting anything." She thanked him, and she and Jax made their way across the hall. After she opened the door, she looked around the room, but she didn't see any package. She pointed towards the closet. "All the outfits in there belong to the theater. The ones hanging on the clothes pole belong to me. I'll pack my personal items from the vanity in my handbag. I wasn't sure if the show would go on. But I guess not. I have no idea what I'm going to do now."

"It's just temporary, Laura," Jax soothed as he gathered her things. "You are far too talented. Plenty of other theaters will be knocking down your door in no time at all."

"I wish," she said, but she wasn't so confident. She turned around to set her handbag on the floor and stopped short. There was a bouquet of gardenias sitting on the top of the vanity. A chill ran through her as she slowly sat down. "Jax? Remember when you first came to the theater and questioned me about Mister Sanders' death?"

He laughed as he grabbed a few more clothes and carefully draped them over his arm. "Yeah, you didn't like me very much."

"No, I didn't. But before you left, you asked me about the gardenia that someone had sent to me during the performance that night. You said that they have a special meaning."

"Every flower has its own meaning, good luck, happiness, gratitude, love. Giving someone a gardenia means they have a secret crush on you." His arms were full, and he turned around. "Why are you bringing that up?"

"At the time, I didn't think much about it. Well, maybe I did, but I figured it was just a strange coincidence. Even when I received another one on Monday, I thought it was odd, yet there didn't seem to be any connection."

He laughed again. "Some people believe there's no such thing as a coincidence." He approached her and saw the flowers. "Where did those come from?"

"I don't know," she said, dazed by the sight of them. "They never come with a card."

"How many have you gotten?"

"Three single ones. And now this."

He laid the clothes over the back of her chair. "When did you get the first one?"

"I was working in the Follies. It was a Friday night, I think, back in March. I shared a dressing room with the rest of the girls, and they all thought it was sweet when it was delivered to me. But then, the stage manager called us all together to tell us about Kitty Cooper's death the prior night."

"And the second one was delivered to you the night after Sam Sanders' death," he stated.

She looked up at him, worriedly. "And Mister Beacham died this past week."

Jax glared at the flowers now. "He was killed sometime last weekend. Joe told me when we stopped at his office. He said that his body was dragged through the woods surrounding the pond and dumped into the water shortly after his death. I wasn't going to bring that up. You said you got one on Monday?"

"It was on my vanity when I arrived for rehearsal. Jax, how did Mister Beacham die?"

He hesitated. "An overdose of chloroform." They both fell silent with their own ugly thoughts.

"So, who sent these flowers to me?" she finally asked. "Robert Ashworth has been in custody since yesterday, and it was delivered an hour ago according to Mister Kratz."

"I don't know, but I'm going to find out." And he disappeared out the door. But within minutes, he returned. "Mister Kratz has no idea who made the delivery, and Jimmy, whoever he is, already left the theater."

"He's one of the stage crew."

"Mister Kratz doesn't have a telephone number for him, but there can't be many flower shops who make deliveries in Manhattan. I'll start making phone calls when we get back to my place."

Quietly, Jax collected Laura's clothes and headed out the door. Laura took one last look inside the room, but her vision was drawn to the bouquet, and she walked away. When they got back to the car, they budged Ace over in the backseat to fit Laura's clothes.

"Jax, we haven't eaten all day, and I'm kind of hungry," she said. "We spent a lot of time at the police station, and it's going on four o'clock already. Can we stop at Roxy's? It's a little diner where the girls and I go for coffee in the morning. They have club sandwiches. My treat. We can bring them back to the apartment if you want."

"I've been there before, but I'll buy," he stated.

She didn't like the abrupt tone of his voice or seeing him so serious, even angry judging by the expression on his face and the way he was clutching the steering wheel. With all that's gone on, she has never seen him this upset. "Are you all right?"

"No, I'm not!" he snapped back, and Ace started barking at him. "I'm not mad at her, Ace. I thought once we had Ashworth and his patsies behind bars, it would all end. But something's not right. There's a piece missing."

She hung her head down, feeling guilty. "I should move back to my place now, Jax. I know you haven't had a good night's sleep the past two days. You're tired and out of sorts, and it's my fault. I'll be fine by myself now that those men are locked up."

He took a deep breath and softened his voice. "You're not going anywhere, Laura. Not yet. Those gardenias are bothering me. Not you or lack of sleep." He looked over with that dimpled grin she'd grown to love, and he winked at her. "Is that better?"

She smiled. "Yes, it is."

Jax picked up three club sandwiches and a couple of sodas. When they got to his apartment, Laura and Ace sat down at the table, but Jax took his sandwich over to the counter. He set it beside the telephone and started dialing and eating at the same time. After the eighth call, he slammed the receiver down.

"Did you know that there are at least twenty floral shops that deliver in Manhattan alone?" he complained as he joined them at the table. "That's what Sylvia just told me. And there are other shops outside the area that deliver to all five boroughs in the city. So that's a brick wall."

"We may be wrong about the gardenias," Laura said. "Maybe we're just jittery and overthinking this because of everything else that's happened. It could simply be an innocent fan sending them. Or they're from Robert Ashworth, which sounds too far-fetched, and he had ordered the delivery before he was arrested. They may even be from my brother, and his timing is just a coincidence. I wouldn't put it past him. He and I were always horsing around and giving each other a hard time. He was constantly teasing me because I wasn't interested in having a relationship with anyone."

Jax's ears perked up. "No sweetheart back home?"

"That depends on who you talk to," she replied flatly.

"Huh. I wonder what that means."

She stood up and grabbed his empty plate. "It means, it's a long story."

"Well, we've got nothing but time right now." She clammed up, so he sat there quietly watching her put the dishes in the sink. "I keep thinking about something you said before."

"I know I'm going to regret asking what that would be."

"Actually, you had made a good point. Sam Sanders' death was more calculating and personal than Kitty Cooper's. I don't want to upset you again by bringing it up, but Horace Beacham was killed in the same manner as Kitty. Using chloroform. If Robert Ashworth was responsible for all three murders, then why did he choose a slower and more painful way to kill Sanders? Despite his relationship with Patricia Sanders, it seems getting his hands on the manuscript was far more important to him."

"And that's a financial motive, not personal," she finished for him. "They haven't been able to find either copy of the manuscript yet, have they?"

"No. So, between that and those gardenias, I'm wondering if there's another player involved who is still out there."

22
Lunch

Saturday, June 9

Jax didn't get a wink of sleep, but not because of any physical discomfort from spending another night on the sofa. Surprisingly, he'd found a fairly comfortable position. But every time he closed his eyes, his mind reeled with a million different thoughts ricocheting from the past to the present and back again. He had been gifted with an extraordinary memory people have told him. Yet, it felt like a curse more often than not.

At dawn, he stood by the window, gazing out at the sun rise. Within the piles upon piles of images and statements stuck in his head, he thought about Laura's comments. How she had refused to become involved with anyone, and the long story behind it. There was no doubt that he was sweet on her. But every time he thought about kissing her or letting her know how he felt, either something disastrous happened, or Tim's statement popped into his head, stopping him cold.

She was definitely out of his league. He knew that for a fact. A week ago, he thought it didn't matter. Yet, whenever these murders were finally solved and the cases were closed, she would go her merry way, and he would go his. It was inevitable for her to become a great star on stage and probably in films, too, with her talent. All the while, he would still be here, unofficially pounding the beat with Tim trying to solve more crimes and struggling to let go of his past. To make things worse, Ace would be heartbroken when they said goodbye and went their separate ways. He'd thought it was terrific that Ace had quickly grown so attached to her. But he wished now that Ace hadn't.

And that he hadn't.

He gazed out the window for another hour before finally heading into the kitchen to make some coffee. As he stood over the stove heating the kettle, he heard Laura come out of the bedroom with Ace beside her, as usual. She said good morning to him and sat down at the table.

"What are you two doing up so early?" he asked.

"Same as you, I think," she replied. "Neither of us slept very well. I wondered if I could give Jeanie a call. I never gave her your telephone number, and she's probably worried sick. Especially if she and Margie read about Mister Beacham in the newspaper. They knew how fond I was of him. I also wanted to give my mother a call, too, if you don't mind. I'm sure she doesn't know anything about all this, but I usually call her a few times a week, and I haven't had a chance."

"Feel free to use the telephone," he said without looking at her again since his previous thoughts were still weighing on his mind. "Coffee will be ready in a minute."

She smiled at him. "I had another thought, too. I don't know what you have planned for the day, but I wondered if I could ask Jeanie and Margie if they're free for lunch? Jeanie would be thrilled, and Margie wants to meet you. We could meet them at Roxy's."

He forced a chuckle. "Lunch with three women? I'd be an idiot to refuse."

"Oh, good. I'm going to call Jeanie right now. She's an early bird."

By noon, Jax and Laura sat together in a booth drinking a couple of sodas. When Jeanie showed up, she told them that Margie was excited and would join them any minute. Then, she mentioned reading about Mister Beacham in the newspaper. After she reached over and cupped Laura's hand sympathetically, she started asking all kinds of questions about what had happened. She was shocked to learn that Robert Ashworth was in custody, and the theater had closed.

"There are open auditions at the Imperial on Monday for a new Broadway play, Laura," Jeanie told her. "I think it starts at one-thirty in the afternoon."

"Thank you, Jeanie. That's encouraging."

"Margie and I are going to the oyster bar at Grand Central for dinner later tonight. Did you and Jax want to join us? We haven't been there in ages, and I'm so looking forward to it."

"That sounds like fun, doesn't Jax?" Laura asked.

"Sure. Will you ladies excuse me for a moment? I want to give Murph a call to see if there are any new developments in the case. I see a pay phone over there. I'll be right back."

Jeanie called out, "Don't be long, Jax! Margie will be here in a flash."

He snickered as he walked away, hearing Jeanie tell Laura what a dreamboat he was. He picked up the telephone receiver, slid the nickel into the slot, and asked the switchboard operator to connect him to Sergeant Murphy at the thirteenth precinct. When Tim answered, he told Jax that both Robert Ashworth and Orin Marino were released on bail, but they had a few flatfoots trailing them. And Missus Ashworth was threatening to sue the city for a wrongful arrest, but that didn't surprise either of them.

While Jax explained to him about the gardenias that Laura had received, he turned around and noticed another woman was standing beside their table talking with Laura and Jeanie. She was a tall, beautiful, blonde woman. But as he studied her, he stopped speaking. His entire body stiffened and a shiver of alarm swept through him. On the other end of the phone, Tim kept asking what was wrong, but Jax wasn't listening.

The woman suddenly glanced over at him, but she immediately turned away.

"I've got to go, Murph." And he hung up the receiver. By the time he made his way back to the table, the woman was walking out the door. He watched her for a moment before he sat down.

"Well, that was strange," Jeanie huffed. "Half an hour ago Margie was free as a bird the entire day. She better not stiff us tonight."

Laura laughed. "She's probably worried I'll try to drag her to the baseball game this afternoon. Oh, Jax, you just missed meeting Margie. She had an appointment she forgot about. She didn't know you were going to be here and felt bad about having to run off."

"That was Margie?" he asked quietly, still staring at the door.

"Well, no matter," Laura said. "Lunch is on me. You, too, Jeanie. But I'll be honest. Nothing compares to Jax's cooking." Her eyes grew wide. "I mean, his sister's cooking." She discreetly nudged Jax with her elbow, but he was deep in thought.

When they finished eating, Laura paid the bill, grabbed the sandwich bag for Ace, and they left the diner. Jeanie told them that she would see them later, and they parted ways.

"I'm such an idiot," Laura spouted as they walked to his car parked around the block. "Did you hear my blunder? Jeanie didn't miss it, that's for sure. She knows I'm staying at your apartment now. That's why she didn't bug me for a phone number or an address. Well, what's done is done." She looked over at Jax. "You've been awful quiet. What did Tim say when you called him?"

"Laura, what's Margie's last name?"

"Parker. Why?"

"She looked familiar," Jax stated. "How well do you know her?"

"Pretty well, I guess. She and Jeanie are tight. They moved in together when they were both in the Follies last fall. I know Margie grew up in the city. Our apartment building isn't far from yours, so you've probably seen her around."

"Yeah, probably."

Jax didn't want Laura to know what was on his mind. He wished he didn't. So, he tried his best to push it aside for now.

He made a few wisecracks about Jeanie's incessant talking, then he told Laura that she seemed like a very nice person. He didn't bring up Margie again, deliberately, and he was glad that Laura had dismissed his questions about her.

As soon as they arrived back at his apartment, Laura gave Ace his sandwich and disappeared into the bedroom. She was excited about going to dinner at the oyster bar tonight and wanted to decide what to wear. Jax, on the other hand, began pacing back and forth across the kitchen floor. His stomach was churning from the gutting thoughts in his head. Sweat dripped down his face, and even his hands were trembling. Then, he stopped dead center in the room.

He knew what he had to do. Yet, it would be like facing the devil and walking through hell again to get to heaven. For a second, he thought about taking the cowardly way out by asking Tim to take care of it, but he didn't want his good friend to come anywhere near his past.

"What do you think, Jax?" Laura asked cheerfully. She stood in the doorway wearing a sleeveless, deep blue velvet dress that was pinned higher on one side with a velvet rose. She spun around so he could see the low-cut back. "Is this too extravagant? I've never been to the oyster bar, but I heard it's incredible."

She was incredible, he wanted to tell her. Just the sight of her instantly shoved all those ill thoughts from his mind, at least for the moment. She was absolutely ravishing. Her short chestnut curls were tousled from trying on different outfits. Her blue-green eyes sparkled, her fair skin looked as soft as the velvet dress, and her sweet smile weakened his senses.

Yet, he just grinned and simply said, "That's a lovely dress. You'll fit right in."

"Don't rat on me," she laughed. "The dress belongs to the theater, and I fell in love with it. I thought I'd borrow it just for a little while and return it later."

"My lips are sealed," he chuckled. But his previous thoughts crashed through. "I never told you what Murph and I talked about on the telephone. He asked me for a favor, something that has to do with another case of his. Would you mind staying here with Ace for an hour or so?"

"No, I guess not."

By her tone, he could tell that she wasn't happy about it, and he approached her. "I won't be long. I promise. Keep an eye on Ace for me."

She feigned a pout. "I'm starting to feel like a prisoner."

"You're not a prisoner, Laura. I'm sorry if you feel that way. You'll be back in your own apartment soon enough."

She lost her playfulness and stared at him. Then, she reached up to touch his cheek. "Jax, what's wrong? There's a look in your eyes that I haven't seen before."

For all the world, he wanted to kiss her. But he couldn't now. Not with the ugly task that awaited him. "Can I wear my rumpled brown suit tonight?"

She shook her head, laughing.

He took her hand in his. "Then, why don't you rummage through my closet and find something for me to wear while I'm gone."

"Okay. Go take care of your detective work. I feel bad making Ace stay here with me."

"Believe me, Ace would rather be with you." So would he, but he forced a laugh and headed out the door.

23
The Orphanage

Jax drove through Manhattan, crossed over the bridge, and headed north along the Hudson River. He slowed the car down a little more every mile he traveled. It was reflex rather than any conscious effort on his part. Yet, as he grew closer to his destination, with every second that ticked by, he was sucked deeper and deeper into his memories. For nine years, he had managed to avoid traveling anywhere north of the city. He swore he never would.

The road veered to the right up ahead. It was only a matter of minutes now. Again, he felt sick to his stomach, and he tightened his grip around the steering wheel to stop his hands from shaking. He turned down the narrow, winding drive which was thickly lined on both sides with mammoth trees stretching overhead, depleting any sunlight. He was entering hell now, and it felt to him as though this time, he would never escape.

When the old building came into view, he desperately wanted to turn the car around. The orphanage was tucked in seclusion along the Hudson River and appeared just as menacing as he remembered from his childhood. He drove up to the main gate and stopped the car. He sat there for a moment to study the mammoth wrought-iron fence surrounding the property.

He couldn't count the number of times that he'd climbed over it, making his escape. Even after they attempted to thwart his efforts by entwining a set of barbed wires around the sharp tips of each iron spindle, he viewed that as a double dare, and his success rate increased. But he noticed the barbed wire had been removed.

He looked at the gate again and was surprised to see that it wasn't closed securely. He got out of the car and wandered over. The large, heavy padlock that he remembered was gone, and he easily pushed the gate open. Finally, he drove up the hill. He parked along the curb in front of the building. He didn't waste any time now. He was anxious to get this over with, so he avoided looking around and headed directly for the main entrance.

After taking a deep breath, he knocked on the door. Then, he waited with his arms rigidly at his side, squeezing his fists open and shut, nervously. A young nun opened the door, and before she said a word, he spouted, "Is Sister Rosemary here?"

"Yes, sir, but she is teaching a class right now. May I help you?"

His vision wandered beyond her, and he fell lost his thoughts.

"Sir? Can I help you with something?"

"Sorry. My name is Jax Diamond. I...I had a few questions that I wanted to ask Sister Rosemary." And preferably right here on the front step, he wanted to tell her.

The nun's eyes light up. "Mister Diamond? Oh, yes, please, come in. I believe she wouldn't mind this interruption. Come in, come in," she urged excitedly.

He didn't question her reaction. He was struggling to find the courage to step inside. Once he did, he stood there stiffly. Yet, he was immediately struck by the fact that the main hallway stretching out ahead of him didn't look as dark and dingy as he remembered.

"Wait here, please." And the nun scurried off.

Within minutes, he saw Sister Rosemary walking down the hall towards him. Her familiar face relaxed him a little. He didn't want to speak with anyone else. Had she been unavailable or no longer here, he undoubtedly would have lost his nerve and high-tailed it back to the city as fast as his car would take him. And without getting any answers to the questions that were gnawing at him.

"Jax Diamond..." Sister Rosemary said with her approach. "You are a sight for sore eyes." Foregoing her traditional greeting, she outstretched her arms welcomingly and hugged him. "My, my. Look at you. All grown up and even more handsome than I remember. When Sister Catherine told me that you were waiting to see me, I couldn't believe my ears."

"It's nice to see you again, Sister Rosemary. You're looking well."

"Better than I feel sometimes," she replied, smiling at him. She wrapped her arm around him, and they walked down the hall together. "I remember the day you were finally permitted to leave the orphanage. You swore that you would never come back, and I didn't blame you one bit. Yet, things have changed drastically in the past few years, and for the better."

"I noticed a few changes down by the gate," he told her.

She laughed. "No padlock to prevent anyone from coming or going, and we removed the barbed wire. Did you notice?"

"I was glad to see it."

"Not that it stopped you from seeking your freedom. A few years ago, Father Patrick was relocated to a convent in Albany, and I was placed in charge. My first priority was concentrating on the lengthy list of improvements that needed to be made. The Sisters and I have been busy ever since. Already, we have completed many of them, although we have a long way to go. All in due time, they say. But you didn't come here to see our renovations, did you? Let us talk privately in my office."

She opened the door at the end of the hall, but Jax hesitated.

"I remember entering this room so many times before to face the inevitable punishment waiting for me."

"That was then, Jax," she told him. "Trust me."

He followed her inside and looked around. The room was bright and cheery with the window wide open rather than tightly covered up with heavy, floor-length drapes. The furniture was different and rearranged. So, too, were the paintings and wall hangings. He noticed another nun in the corner, straightening up. Sister Rosemary called her over to them.

"Sister Mary Helen, this is Jax Diamond," Sister Rosemary introduced.

"Oh, my. It is very nice to meet you, sir."

"You are quite a legend around here, Jax," Sister Rosemary said. "I hope you don't mind, but I have shared some of your stories not only with the sisters who weren't here to witness them but the children as well. I wanted everyone to understand fully that the orphanage was no longer a place to be feared, but a friendly and loving home where the children can learn, play, and grow up happy and healthy."

Jax sat on the sofa after the other nun left the room, and Sister Rosemary sat beside him rather than behind her desk. "I was hoping you could give me some information about another resident who was here for a few years before I left," he began. "Do you remember Wanda Dillenbeck?"

Sister Rosemary lost her smile. "Well, there is a name I hoped to never hear again. You know I believe there is good in every child despite some of their behaviors, which is why I had such faith in you, Jax. Although I certainly favored you above the others since I was the one who discovered you on the doorstep and gave you a name. I do wish that I could have done much more for you, though. I know how unhappy you were here, but my hands were tied."

"I don't fault you for anything, Sister Rosemary. There were plenty of times you came to my rescue."

"Perhaps." She waited a moment, thinking about his question. "Not surprisingly, Wanda and her brother had spent most of their lives in one facility or another. Wanda's tactics were underhanded and vicious, to be honest. I dislike speaking ill of anyone. But unlike you fighting for your own survival, she found some sort of pleasure or glory in the suffering of others. Quite deliberately, she would destroy property or hurt another child, then manipulate the situation and those around her so that she was never to blame. It would have been heartbreaking had she not done so much damage or seemed to rejoice in it afterward."

"I didn't realize you were aware of what she was doing," he told her.

She stood up now in remembrance. "There were a few of us who spoke with Father Patrick about it when we witnessed it for ourselves. He always saw it differently, though, and chastised us for suggesting that she was a wicked child. Yet, that was the perfect word to describe her."

"Do you know what happened to her and her brother?"

"They were both transferred to the institution in Poughkeepsie shortly after you left. Less than a year later, we were told that they had both died in a tragic drowning accident during an outing by the river. I paid penance after hearing about it in hopes of absolving my guilt from thoughts of relief."

"I heard about the accident and just assumed that they were still living here at the time. So, you wouldn't have any sort of record detailing the events of that day?"

"I'm afraid not." She sat down beside him again. "I heard you quit the police force and became a private detective. Oh, yes, Jax, I have kept track of you, and I have sung your praises whenever the opportunity arose. I understand your confidentiality policy, but I do wonder why you are here asking about Wanda?"

"You have been more than kind, Sister Rosemary. Frankly, I was terrified about coming here today as you probably guessed. I'm glad I did. It is very good seeing you again and the changes you've made. This place doesn't hold the same cold feeling that I remember, which means the setting of my nightmares is gone. For that, I am eternally grateful to you."

"I feel blessed that we have crossed paths again, Jax. Before you leave, there is one thing I would like to show you. It will only take a moment." He followed her out of the office and down another hallway. She opened the outer door that led to the backyard. "We received several generous donations for a new playground."

Outside, two dozen children were playing and laughing and having a grand time together. He watched them for a while, smiling now. With each change that he saw, a rotten memory disappeared. "Bless you, Sister Rosemary."

"Sister Margarita is over there, pushing Sonia on the swings. She is the aunt of a young boy who died tragically two years ago. I believe you will remember him. Jonah Rivera."

The name jolted him and stole his breath.

"Jonah and his mother were taken hostage during a bank robbery on the Lower East Side," Sister Rosemary stated. "The first policeman on the scene was given strict instructions not to interfere until his superior and fellow officers arrived. Had he disobeyed his orders, he would have been immediately dismissed from the force in disgrace." She wrapped her arm around him again. "It must have been quite a struggle for you trying to decide what to do in such a volatile situation. I imagine your only thought was to find a way inside the bank to rescue them both. But according to Jonah's mother, their abductor had already killed Jonah by the time you arrived and because you followed orders, they were able to save her life. Sister Margarita knew your name, from the stories I had told her. She said that she and her family view you as a hero for alerting the police of their whereabouts and saving the life of her sister."

Jax turned to her and hugged her tightly. She held him close and was glad that she had given him comfort.

"Jax, there is nothing that you have ever done in your life that is deserving of the guilt that I know has been tormenting you," she whispered to him. "I do not know where you came from or who your parents were, but I do know this. They must have been two extremely loving, selfless, and determined souls who truly believed that your life at the orphanage would be better than with them. As wrong as that seems to you, trust their reasons just as strongly as you trust your own instincts. Perhaps, they saved your life."

He pulled away to look at her then. The fact that she had referenced both of his parents gave him the sense that she knew more than what she said. And by the look in her dark-brown eyes, he could tell that she either wouldn't or couldn't divulge anything further.

Yet, she had just given him the greatest gift of all.

24

Grand Central Terminal

Jax drove down the hill after he left the orphanage. He grinned smugly as he passed through the open gate, and for a while, he relished in all that he had seen and mostly, what he'd learned. It felt to him as though he had just broken free of the heavy chains that had bound him for years. He knew it would take time for him to fully absorb everything Sister Rosemary had told him. His mind had been so conditioned into thinking the worst of his past and himself. But already, he could breathe easier.

He traveled at a faster speed due to his high spirits. He was also anxious to see Laura. If she were here with him right now, he would do exactly what was on his mind before he left and kiss her. He didn't care what the future held for them, or that they would undoubtedly part ways when this case was closed. He just wanted to savor in how glad he was that they had even met.

It wasn't until he reached the city limits and drove through Manhattan that he thought about Wanda Dillenbeck again. He was just a kid when he knew her. Or rather when he first met her and started keeping his distance from her. Calling her wicked was right on the mark. Even an understatement. He doubted that Sister Rosemary was fully aware of half of the diabolical schemes that Wanda had cooked up and implemented.

Back then, Wanda appeared to be a sweet and innocent young girl with freckles and vibrant red hair pulled back in a long ponytail. The perfect, obedient child who showered those in charge of the orphanage with adoration and gratitude, especially Father Patrick. Yet, behind their backs, she was planning and plotting with her younger brother, who was nothing more than her personal puppet.

It was Wanda's green eyes that had first alerted him to steer clear of her. They weren't a deep and dazzling bluish-green like Laura's. Wanda's were lighter in color, nearly transparent at times. Especially when she had some devious prank on her mind. Within the first month after her arrival, alone, little Tommy Bean had been severely punished for breaking an upstairs window, throwing an egg at Sister Augusta, and his arm was in a sling after clumsily tripping down the stairs.

Once, and only once, Jax had been Wanda's target, but he put an end to that quick. The trouble was, it became difficult for him to protect the younger kids from her vicious tricks without catching the blame, himself.

When he'd heard that Wanda and her brother had drowned, he felt as much if not more relief than Sister Rosemary. At the time, he assumed that it was the siblings' comeuppance, payback by a group of the other kids at the orphanage who'd had enough of their antics.

Until he knew without a shadow of a doubt that Wanda and her brother's bodies had been dredged from the Hudson River, he wouldn't rest. Margie looked far too similar to Wanda, grown-up, and he still swears that it was her brother who had been following them at Coney Island. Although tonight, he and Laura were having dinner with Margie, and it was the perfect opportunity for him to study her appearance and demeanor, which could confirm the matter one way or another.

Jax hurried up the stairs to his apartment when he got home. He unlocked the door and found Laura sitting on the couch with Ace. She was reading one of his books from the shelf. She smiled when she saw him and slammed the book shut.

"What took you so long, Jax? You've been gone over two hours! Ace and I were getting bored and running out of things to do."

He walked over to her, snatched her hand, and pulled her to her feet. He wrapped his other arm about her waist and twirled her around as though dancing. "We're going out on the town tonight, Ace."

She was laughing, too. "What's gotten into you?"

"Oh, I don't know. I feel like I'm on top of the world." He stopped and gazed at her beautiful face. "What time are we meeting your friends?"

"Six o'clock, so we should leave in about an hour. I found a nice grey suit in your closet for you to wear, along with a light blue shirt and tie. They will bring out those baby blues of yours, Detective." She stood on her tiptoes and pecked him on the cheek. "We're going to have fun tonight, Jax. I'll get dressed first." She headed into the bedroom, then peeked over at him. "You could use a shave."

He stood there smiling at her until she disappeared. Then, he glanced over at Ace, winked at him, and went to clean up.

Jax parked the car on Forty-Second Street, and they walked to the main entrance of Grand Central Terminal. As they approached the front doorways, they admired the large arched windows above the doors that were surrounded by beautiful granite sculptures of the Roman Gods, Minerva, Hercules, and Mercury.

The main concourse of the building stretched from Forty-Second Street in the south to Forty-Fifth Street in the north and was swarming with travelers, sightseers, and shoppers. The clatter and clamor filled the wide hall and bounced off the eighty-four-foot arched ceilings. Laura told Jax that the only time she had been to the terminal was when she had first arrived. But simply being the city had been too overwhelming, so she was thrilled to have a chance to take a closer look inside such an extraordinary landmark.

Jax admitted that no matter how many times he'd been there, he was still amazed at the intricate network of tunnels and passages. They branched off in every direction, leading to the railroad terminals on the main level, and the lower level ramps. Then, there were dozens of short stairways climbing to the elevated terrace that encircled the entire building.

Laura didn't want to keep her friends waiting, so they headed down the ramp to the lower-level dining areas. Just before the restaurant's entrance, they passed through the Whispering Gallery, a wide ceramic archway. Jax played a game with Laura. He told her to stand with her back to him in one corner of the arch, then he hurried over to the opposite corner, a good distance away, and did the same. She didn't understand what he was up to, but she went along with it.

As he stood there with his back to her, he spoke quietly. "You look absolutely stunning this evening, Laura." He slowly turned around to see if she'd heard him.

She peeked over at him with such a sweet smile on her face. "It sounded like you were right beside me!" she squealed.

"There's a whole lengthy acoustical explanation why you could hear what I said from such a distance," he told her. "I think it's pretty nifty."

"And thank you for the compliment, Jax. You look very handsome tonight."

He wrapped her arm in his and escorted her into the restaurant.

Jeanie had arrived and was waiting for them at one of the tables. "I love your dress, Laura! Hello again, Jax.

He nodded to her, pulled out the chair for Laura, and they sat down.

"Isn't this place fantastic!" Jeanie exclaimed. "It's like a city within a city. Margie and I get such a kick out of watching everyone, people strolling around while others are rushing to catch their trains. We stopped in the new shoe store upstairs, and Margie ran into someone she knew, so she'll be right along."

"This is a lovely restaurant," Laura said as she glanced around.

"They have terrific seafood, if I remember," Jax commented. "I think clam chowder is one of their specialties."

"Don't forget about their scrumptious oysters." And Jeanie chattered on, bouncing from one subject to another with barely a breath in between. The waiter stopped by their table, and Jeanie explained they were waiting for one more person.

Laura suddenly stood up. "Will you both excuse me? I see the restrooms down the hall, and I'd like to freshen up. Jeanie, could you keep Jax company for a few minutes?"

Jeanie smiled at him. "I'd be happy to."

Jax flashed Laura a pleading look, begging her not to leave him alone, but she laughed and assured him that she would be right back. He watched her leave and turned his chair slightly so he could keep her in sight until she disappeared into the restroom. All the while, Jeanie rattled on about this and that while his mind wandered.

It seemed less and less likely to him that Margie wasn't who she claimed to be. It made much more sense that she just happened to look a lot like Wanda. After all, Jeanie had lived with Margie since last fall, and Laura had known her since March. Neither of them had mentioned noticing any unusual behavior from their friend. So, maybe he was just reaching for straws with another far-fetched hunch. Still, no matter what he ended up deciding after he met Margie, he intended to ask Tim to try and get his hands on the police report regarding the drowning in Poughkeepsie.

Jax saw a few women leave the restroom, along with someone in a wheelchair, but they all headed back to the concourse. Even though Laura had only been gone a few minutes, Jeanie continued jabbering on, and it seemed like hours. He pretended to be listening to her, mindlessly nodding his head now and then, yet he kept his eyes peeled on the hallway. Then, he remembered Tim complaining about the amount of time Carla spent 'freshening up' when the three of them went out to dinner. So, he leaned back in his chair and tried to relax.

But more time passed, and he watched several other women enter and leave the restroom. "Excuse me, Jeanie," he said, cutting her off. "Would you mind checking on Laura? I don't want to sound impatient, but it seems as though she's been gone for some time."

"I didn't even notice," she told him. "Margie isn't here yet either. I'm going to give her a piece of my mind when she finally joins us."

Jax sat upright in his seat now, nervously. He watched Jeanie walk down the hall and enter the restroom. Within seconds, she came out the door. She quickly looked behind her towards the lower concourse. Then, she turned towards him, lifted her arms, and shrugged her shoulders.

Jax panicked and bolted out of the restaurant.

"She's not in there in, Jax," Jeanie told him as he flew by her.

He shoved the door open. "Laura! Laura!" But there was no response.

He ignored the squeals of the other women and rushed inside to check for himself. Then he darted past Jeanie again to search the lower level. He raced through the crowds of people in one direction, then he spun around and rushed in the other direction, shouting Laura's name over and over again. People stopped and stared at him as though he were crazy, but he was beside himself. His heart was pounding in fear, and he couldn't catch his breath.

Finally, he stopped for a second, closed his eyes, and tried to think it through.

There were only two ramps that led upstairs. Yet, they were at either end of the concourse that spread three-quarters of a mile. He focused on the closest ramp and wasted no time. He was hysterical and kept calling her name as he made his way up the ramp until he came to the main concourse. He didn't know what to do, where to look next. The only thing he did know was that someone had taken her from that restroom by force. And there were dozens of passageways, too many for him to search by himself.

He saw a security guard and rushed over to him. "Call the police!" he yelled at him. "I'm Detective Diamond. Someone was abducted. Get the police down here right away!"

"Excuse me, sir?" the guard asked.

"I said call the police!"

He swore under his breath and ran over to the pay phone on the wall. He fumbled around trying to find a nickel in his pocket and several other coins fell to the floor with a few rolling away. He called Tim at home and struggled trying calm down long enough to explain what had happened. As soon as Tim assured him that he'd send a unit of men there, Jax hung up.

He looked around, trying to get ahold of himself. But on the floor in front of him, he caught sight of a coin that he'd dropped. It was a penny with the head side up. He stared at it for a second, swallowing hard to control his emotions. Then, he bent down, snatched it, and put it into his pocket.

Within half an hour, he was pacing across the sidewalk just outside the front entrance. Tim stood nearby, watching him. "Stan gave Jeanie a ride home, and he's bringing Ace back with him. We have officers at every exit in the station with dozens more searching inside. We're doing all we can, Jax. Who the heck did this?"

He was far too upset to think straight and kept running his hand through his hair, trying to clear his head. He was out of his mind with worry and rage and couldn't settle down long enough to figure out how someone had abducted her right under his nose. Let alone who the culprit was.

He recalled sitting in the restaurant watching the hallway, waiting for Laura to come back to the table. He tried to envision the women who had gone in and out of the restroom. He always prided himself on his impeccable memory. Yet, it was all a blurry mess in his head as images of Laura suffering or worse kept flashing through his mind.

"A wheelchair!" He swung around to face Tim. "Someone left the restroom pushing a wheelchair. That's how they took her out of the restroom without anyone noticing." He charged towards the door. "We need to get back in there and search for anyone in a wheelchair, Murph. Alert the other officers right away."

25
Gone

Three hours later, Tim found Jax and Ace sitting in a back stairwell at the station. There was nothing he could do or say right now that would ease his friend's heartache and worry. As he watched him, there was no doubt in his mind now that Jax had fallen hard for Laura. They've worked plenty of tough cases together the past five years, several involving extremely beautiful women. Yet, Jax has always maintained his distance, a strictly business relationship with all of them. Even when the women hotly pursued him.

Outside of work, he'd dated a few women, and Carla tried fixing him up with a few of her friends, but he had never taken any of them to Duke's Club to share that part of himself. Jax had never opened up to anyone, except for him and his family, until now.

Tim saw Ace by his friend's feet, laying there still tuckered out. He had to give Ace tremendous credit. As soon as Stan dropped him off at the station, he had caught Laura's scent in the restroom, trailed it through the lower level concourse, and up the ramp. But he lost it somewhere on the main level. Still, the devoted and determined pup spent a couple of hours trying to pick up her scent again, as though he knew exactly what had occurred and was just as scared and frantic as Jax. The two of them had traveled the entire length of the terminal, checking every passageway, tunnel, and exit, without any luck.

"There are plenty of men still looking for her inside the station," Tim told him. "I've also alerted every precinct from here to the Lower East Side, and Queens right down through to Coney Island."

"What about the railroad?" Jax muttered. "They could have taken her on one of the trains."

"We're checking every departure, Jax. Someone boarding a train in a wheelchair would be tough to miss. Why don't you and Ace head back to your apartment for a while? There's nothing more you can do here."

"We're not going home without her!"

Tim sighed. He knew Jax wouldn't agree to it, but it was worth a shot. He made his way down the steps and sat beside him. "We both know that this caper took far too much effort and planning to be a random kidnapping. Robert Ashworth is out on bail. A couple of days ago I would have been convinced that he was behind this since Laura was the only other person with a copy of that manuscript. But we didn't find anything in his possession. Besides, he has a whole slew of different legal problems right now, too many for him to risk taking this kind of a chance."

"I'm trying to calm down long enough to think this through, Murph. But she keeps getting in the way, images of her, what she's going through, and how I let all this happen. I knew she was a target. Those gardenias alerted me to that. I shouldn't have let her out of my sight until everything was resolved and the criminals were behind bars. But she was just so excited about coming here for dinner tonight, I couldn't disappoint her."

"Jax, you're too close to this. So often, it seems like you're way out in left field, but more times than not, you're the first one back to home plate. Think of this as just another case to solve right now. That's the best thing you can do for her."

He sat there awhile longer, silently. Then he whispered, "I told Laura that there had to be another player involved. That was right after she found the bouquet of gardenias in her dressing room and informed me about the others."

"Did you ever find out which floral shop sent the deliveries to her at the theater?"

Jax shook his head, struggling to piece this together. "The lilies we found at the crime scenes tie the three murders together. All of the victims worked at the Ambassador Theater, so that's another connection between them. Laura is the third link."

"Laura was acquainted with Sanders and Beacham, but wasn't she working with the Follies at a different theater when Kitty was killed? Did they know each other?"

"Laura was chosen as Kitty's replacement in the current musical after her death."

"So, she knew each of the victims either directly or indirectly."

Jax lifted his head and stared at the wall in front of him. "Laura received a gardenia after each murder. Those flowers were sent as a symbol of admiration, not death." He slowly got to his feet, and so did Ace. "Murph, the man who planned this is in love with Laura. A secret admirer. He doesn't intend to kill her, not yet anyway. But he's not working alone. There had to be a woman waiting in the restroom who drugged Laura or something and put her in that wheelchair."

"Do you think Ashworth is behind it?"

"No. Not him. Laura's friend, Margie, didn't show up for dinner, but she was here at the station. Cripes, Murph, I know who took Laura." That feeling of alarm swept through him again, the same one that he felt when he recognized Margie at the diner. "There isn't time to explain the whole thing to you right now. Just follow us back to Laura's apartment building in Brooklyn."

Jax drove like a maniac through Manhattan to the Lower East Side and across the Williamsburg Bridge into Brooklyn. He wasn't even paying attention to see if Tim was still behind him in his patrol car. He pulled in front of the building and by the time he shut off his engine, Tim pulled behind him.

"What are we doing here?" Tim asked.

"Jeanie and Margie live down the hall from Laura," Jax told him as they entered the building. "I never met Margie before, but when I was talking to you on the phone during lunch today, I saw her. She looked just like someone I knew years ago. At the time, I couldn't be sure it was her. But she recognized me, too. That's why she hightailed it out of the diner. Her name isn't Margie Parker. It's Wanda Dillenbeck. I knew her and her brother years ago when I lived at the orphanage. She's a lunatic, Murph. If she refuses to tell me where Laura is, you'd better arrest her before I kill her." Both he and Ace shot up the stairs to the second floor, but Ace slowed his pace when they passed by Laura's apartment. "Down here, Ace."

It was going on eleven o'clock at night and the hallway was dark, but Jax could see a light shining under their doorway. He knocked and waited impatiently. Just as he lifted his fist to knock again, the door opened just a crack. When Jeanie saw it was him, she let him in.

"Oh, Jax, please tell me that you found Laura and she's okay," Jeanie cried.

"I wish I could. Where is your roommate? Where is Margie!" he shouted at her when she didn't respond right away.

"I...I don't know. She hasn't been home. I thought she might still be at Grand Central waiting to hear about Laura. You don't think she's missing, too, do you?"

"No, she's not missing. I'm sure she's just fine. Which bedroom is hers?"

"Jax, can I have a word with you?" Tim asked.

"Don't lecture me about search warrants now, Murph! I don't want to hear it. Jeanie, who room is Margie's?"

"The second one," she said, pointing towards the hallway. Then, she hurried after him. "What is it, Jax? Why do you want to look in Margie's room?"

He was too furious to answer, and he didn't know himself.

He was just hoping to find something, anything that would give him a clue as to where Margie and her brother took Laura. As soon as he opened the door, Ace ran inside. Jax stormed around searching her vanity and dresser. He tossed all her garments on the floor to make sure nothing was hidden underneath while Ace was frantically sniffing around.

Jax headed over to the closet. He started yanking clothes off the hangers, but he stopped when he saw a shoebox tucked in the far corner of the shelf above him. He pulled it out and threw the top off. It was filled with cutout newspaper articles. He turned around and set the box on the bed. Then, he started sifting through each of them.

He looked over at Tim, who was holding Jeanie now, trying to calm her down and stop her from crying. "These are all the articles and reviews that had been written up about Laura, dating back to January after she arrived in the city." He held up one of them. "This was the first review when the New York Times nicknamed her, 'Songbird'." He looked at the paper again with his stomach in knots. "Murph, send a couple of officers over here. She'll be back eventually."

26
Unhinged

Jimmy opened the back door of his apartment wearing rubber gloves and carrying a watering can. He walked around the rooftop terrace that he'd conformed into a homemade greenhouse, whistling a cheery tune from the musical, and feeling pretty proud of himself. He had outsmarted his sister. The second time ever.

There probably would be hell to pay as soon as she caught wind of it. But for now, he was pleased as punch. All his life she has egged him into doing things her way rather than his own, as though he couldn't think for himself or come up with a clever way to accomplish the deed. Too many times, her ideas had put him smack dab in the middle, and he ended up dangerously close to getting caught and punished while she sat on the sidelines, shining like a rainbow. And it had always been his own quick thinking that got him out of the scrape rather than her shrewdness.

Maybe it was her idea to plan their phony demise back at the institution. But it was her fault when that little girl got in the crossfire of one of their pranks and ended up in the hospital. She didn't survive, but at the time, they figured it was only a matter of hours before the little girl told the authorities who was behind it. So, he took care of the rest.

He chose the perfect scapegoats since the Berkley twins, a brother and sister duo, had the exact same hair color and built as they did. While his sister planted some damning evidence in the twins' bedroom, he lured them down to the river, killed them, changed them into his and his sister's clothing, and dumped them over the cliff into the rushing waters. Then, he and his sister disappeared. Weeks later, they heard that the police had found the bodies and were looking for the Berkley twins as the perpetrators. It was genius and worked like a charm.

Jimmy heard someone pounding on his front door and smiled. He made his way back inside. "Coming!" He unlocked the door, and Margie burst inside like a raging bull.

"Where is she!"

"Quiet, you'll wake up the neighbors," he told her.

Margie ignored him and stormed across the room to the terrace. "Are you keeping her out here, Jimmy? I want to know what you did with her!"

He popped open a bottle of soda. "Did you want a drink, *Wanda*?"

She charged back into the room and got in his face. "No, I don't want a drink! And don't call me that! Tell me what you did with her, Jimmy. I know you didn't kill her as I told you to. Once you took her from the terminal, you were supposed to head east and dump her in the river. You drove south!"

He lost his temper now and pointed a finger at her. "I have done your bidding for twenty-two years now! I never once talked back to you or denied you anything. I have deliberately hurt other kids, killed two of them, and murdered a few others to stay in your good graces. The only thing I have ever asked in return is for you to let me take care of Laura in my own way."

She stood there glaring at him, breathing so heavily, it looked like she was ready to burst. Then, in a flash, she smiled and softened her tone. "We've always been as thick as thieves, Jimmy. Didn't we promise each other that we would stick together no matter what?" She wandered around the room, cool and calm. "I know it's been killing you watching Jax Diamond, of all people, make the moves on the girl of your dreams. Then, Laura moves in with him after you searched her apartment. That has to be eating you up alive." She peeked over at him. "I told you, sometimes murder is necessary. Other times, the best revenge is killing the people closest to them. Think about how crushed Jax will be when he finds out that she's dead."

He gulped the rest of his soda down.

"Tell me where she is, Jimmy," she said sweetly. "I'll take care of it for you this time."

"Leave me alone. I don't want to talk about it." He walked away from her, silently counted backward from six, knowing that's how long it would take for her to explode again.

"She doesn't deserve to live!" Margie screamed at him. "I was the one next in line for Kitty's part after we killed her. That was the whole point of it. But that witch weaseled her way into the lead without a drop of blood and sweat that the rest of us go through to work our way to the top. Then, Samuel Sanders writes a play for her, like she's some sort of goddess. I knew she was trouble the minute I met her. Wake up, little brother! She doesn't give a rat's ass about you. You're just some stupid stagehand."

He swung around, glaring at her now. "Shut-up. I already took care of it!"

She backed away from him, smiling again. "So, you *did* kill her. Tell me how you did it, Jimmy. I want to hear every gooey detail."

Jax and Ace left Tim and the other officers in Jeanie's apartment and slowly walked down the hall. They both stopped in front of Laura's door for a minute, then they climbed down the stairs and went outside.

Jax stood on the sidewalk, not knowing what to do next.

It was almost midnight, six hours after Laura had disappeared. Tim had agreed to have a couple of officers dig around for someone named James Dillenbeck in the city, but he knew it was useless. If Wanda had changed her name, her brother did, too. So, they could be anywhere. Tim was also going to have his men check out all the flower shops to see if they could pinpoint which one delivered the gardenias, and who had sent them. But the shops wouldn't open until morning.

Tim approached him. "The officers parked around the corner so Margie or Wanda wouldn't see them when she comes back to her apartment. And they have their orders to arrest her."

"*If* she comes back here," Jax muttered.

"You only told me a little bit about her, Jax, and you don't have to get into all of it right now, but are you sure that she took Laura?"

"Positive. Like I said, when I saw her briefly at lunch today, she looked familiar. So, I drove to the orphanage where I grew up. Wanda and her brother had lived there for two years, but I heard they both died in some drowning accident in the Hudson not long after I left. I was hoping that someone at the orphanage would have a copy of the police records explaining their deaths. I needed to be sure that they really did drown. I swore I would never go back to that orphanage, Murph."

"That had to be hard for you."

"Sister Rosemary is in charge of it now, and she's done such remarkable things there. She even ended up resolving the issues of my past if you can believe that. Anyway, she said that Wanda and Jimmy had been sent to the institution in Poughkeepsie, and that's where they supposedly died. She didn't know anything more than that."

"I'll call the person in charge of it tomorrow and request those records," Tim said. "Since Wanda and her brother didn't die, that means two other kids did."

"I knew they were both devious. I should have done something to stop them back then. None of this would have happened."

"What could you have done, Jax? You were just a kid."

"Yeah, I guess. I would bet my last buck that they were responsible for cutting my car brakes at the ballpark. They're the ones who wanted me out of the way. But at that point, they weren't out to hurt Laura. They couldn't know that she would be with me after the game."

"Thank goodness, she was."

Jax let out a sad chuckle. "You should've seen her, Murph. She knew exactly what to do and kept her head through the whole thing. She even made a wisecrack after the car had stopped." He lifted his head and stared at the moon shining above them amid a myriad of twinkling stars. It reminded him of the night that he walked Laura home after leaving Tim's apartment. That was the day they had spent together at Coney Island. "God, where is she?"

"We'll find her, Jax."

"At the amusement park last week, I thought I was losing my mind when I saw Jimmy Dillenbeck standing behind Laura. But I wasn't imagining it. Ace had better sense. Without even knowing the man, he knew Jimmy was up to no good and chased after him to get him away from Laura. I wish Ace had caught up to him now, but he probably gave up his pursuit because he didn't want to leave Laura alone."

"He's smarter than the both of us combined, and one hell of a good partner."

Jax looked at Ace, sitting by his side. "We both need her back, Murph."

"I know."

Ace was suddenly on his feet, growling.

Jax looked down the street and saw someone standing in the shadows. When the person ran in the opposite direction, Ace darted off, barking viciously. Jax and Tim rushed after him. They heard a woman scream and quickened their pace. Just before the corner, they saw Ace pounce on the woman and knock her down. And he stood over her, snarling, while she kept squealing and cursing, and trying to cover her face with her handbag.

Jax saw it was Margie. "Good work, Ace." He grabbed Margie's arm and yanked her to her feet. Then, he pushed her back against the brick wall and shoved his forearm over her throat. "Where is Laura? Tell me right now, or I'll strangle every breath from you!"

Tim pulled him away. "That's enough, Jax."

Margie doubled over, coughing and choking, but Jax knew she was exaggerating since he hadn't put any pressure on her neck.

Tim roughly turned her around and handcuffed her wrists together. "I'll take her to the station and do this the legal way." He led her to his car and pushed her into the back seat.

At the precinct in one of the interview rooms, Jax stood in the corner while Tim and Lieutenant Simmons questioned Margie. He'd only been allowed into the room as long as he promised not to interfere. So, he impatiently leaned against the wall with his arms folded in front of him while Ace sat beside him, watchfully.

After an hour, they had gotten nowhere. Margie had admitted being at Grand Central Terminal when the police began swarming the place. She heard someone had been abducted, and she claimed to have gotten trapped within the crowds leaving the building. So, she took a taxi to her boyfriend's nightclub and spent the next several hours there. She pretended to look shocked when they told her that Laura was missing. She even pulled a handkerchief out of her handbag to wipe her fretting tears away.

Next, they questioned her about Wanda Dillenbeck, and her entire demeanor changed. She appeared puzzled and told them that she had no idea who that was. She denied having a younger brother and said she grew up on Long Island with her two older sisters. She even offered their names. And she went on about her family, how they moved to California a few years ago while she decided to stay behind to pursue her acting career.

Throughout this conversation, she spoke calmly, nonchalantly, as though she didn't have a care in the world and was just chatting with a few friends. Deliberately, she focused on the Lieutenant during the entire interrogation and avoided any eye contact with Jax.

"We'll need to get in touch with your family, so if you wouldn't mind writing their information down," the Lieutenant told her, and he slid a pad and pencil across the table.

"She's lying," Jax stated coldly. He ignored the other men's protests, came forward, and rested his hands on the table. Then, he leaned in and looked Margie dead in the eye. "All they have to do is make one simple phone call to Sister Rosemary at the orphanage near Englewood. I'm sure the good Sister would be more than happy to tell them exactly who you are and where you came from."

There it was. He'd struck a nerve. The color of her eyes instantly washed away as she glared at him, and he knew if she had a knife in her hand right now, she would drive it through his heart. Ace knew it too and began growling. Even Tim and Lieutenant Simmons fell silent.

She sat back in the chair, grinning. "Jax Diamond. We meet again after all these years. With all the cops in the city, it was just my brother's dumb luck that you started poking around. Although, I think he's been enjoying playing cat and mouse with you again, especially since he's kept one step ahead of you."

"Until now."

"Oh, I think he is still way ahead, isn't he, Jax?" She started to stand up to put some space between him and her, but Ace moved forward, menacingly, and kept her in her seat.

"So, you're blaming your brother for all of it?"

She placed her hand over her heart. "Oh, but of course. I could never commit murder. I was afraid of what he would do to me if I didn't go along with him. He has a ferocious temper, and he's constantly threatening me."

Jax grew impatient. "Tell me where Laura is!"

"Ah, Laura," she cackled. "The source of all these wicked deaths and the love of your life, right, Jax? Jimmy was none too pleased watching the two of you grow closer. The last thing he wanted to do was hurt her, but because of you, he had no other choice." She stared at him with those cold green eyes. "He killed her, Jax."

He stormed out of the room with Ace. He couldn't breathe and leaned against the wall to support himself. She was a liar, he kept telling himself over and over again. None of this was her brother's idea. Every dastardly deed those two had ever committed had been her idea, not her brother's. He was just a puppet, a tool she'd used to achieve her demented goals.

He suddenly pushed himself upright. "Ace, she called her brother Jimmy." At the theater, Mister Kratz had said that Jimmy signed for the bouquet of gardenias and put them in Laura's dressing room.

A stagehand had full access to the theater, including both Robert Ashworth's office and Mister Beacham's files. He also had the perfect opportunity to deliver Sam Sanders dinner to him on the day of his death, after he poisoned the man's meal.

Margie had obviously hated Laura and was jealous as hell over her success. Had she confessed to doing the killing, it might be true. But Jimmy was in love with Laura, so killing her would be no easy task.

27
Berries

Sunday, June 10, 3:00 am

Laura woke up. She was laying on a cold, hard surface, and it was pitch dark in the room. Her head was pounding and her mouth was so dry, she could barely swallow. She tried to sit up, but she grew dizzy from the effort. Even with her eyes acclimated to the darkness, she couldn't see anything as though she had fallen into a black abyss.

She leaned back against a wall and closed her eyes, trying to remember what had happened. She pictured Jax and Jeanie sitting with her at the table in the restaurant. The waiter had stopped and asked if they were ready to order. That's when she saw Margie in the hallway, smiling and motioning to her. And she pressed her index finger over her lips as though she wanted to tell her some exciting secret. But after she had followed her into the restroom, Margie pushed her into one of the cubicles.

Laura began rubbing her temples, trying to stop the painful throbbing so she could remember what happened after that, and understand why Margie had looked so angry with her.

She finally got to her feet, using the wall behind her for support. She was in some sort of room and every room had an exit. Yet, not knowing what was in front of her, she kept one hand on the wall to guide her way around. When her foot hit something solid, she bent down to see if she could feel what it was to help her determine where she was. Within a few minutes, she realized it was some sort of storage room. Boxes were stacked around the perimeter, some filled with metal objects. Others were stuffed with coarse and silky fabrics, feathers, beads, and additional trinkets. Props, she realized, like the ones they use at the theater.

She continued her search until she came upon an indentation in the wall that stretched above her head and to the floor. Excitedly, she found the doorknob. It was locked, but she kept turning it both ways using every bit of her strength as though it would miraculously open. She felt around for a window, but it was one solid mass.

She pounded her fists against the door, screaming at the top of her lungs until her voice went hoarse and her hands went numb. She started to cry, then shook the emotion off knowing it would do no good. She needed to keep her head so she could find a way out of this.

She thought about Jax then, and how clever he was. Despite the odds against him, he had doggedly pursued his suspicions about Mister Sanders' death, and she knew in her heart that he wouldn't stop until he found her. She may not remember what had happened in the restroom, but he had only been sitting a short distance away. It wouldn't take him long to figure it all out. That assurance eased her mind a little until a noise startled her.

Someone was on the other side of the door, unlocking it. She backed away carefully so as not to trip on anything behind her. As the door creaked open, a light filtered into the room, illuminating it. She saw the lantern first. Next, she saw a person's hand gripping a knife.

"Laura?" he called out.

She nearly screamed with joy when she recognized his voice. "Jimmy! Thank heavens you found me!" She ran to him and hugged him tightly with tears streaming down her cheeks. "I don't know how I got here, or why someone brought me here. I don't even know where we are! The theater, I think." He held her close yet remained silent.

She finally loosened her embrace. "Jimmy?"

"Sit down, Laura," he said, flashing the knife at her, and he quickly locked the door. "We need to talk."

"I don't understand, Jimmy," she said as she sat down on one of the boxes, stunned. "What are you doing?"

"Saving your life." He pulled the satchel from around his shoulder and placed that, the lantern, and the set of keys on the floor. All the while, he held the knife in full view. Then, he sat down on the cardboard box beside her. "My sister has been wanting me to kill you ever since you were given the lead in Blossom Time instead of her."

It took her a moment to comprehend his words. "Margie wanted that part. She's your sister?" As horrifying as that was, it was the only thing that made sense of how she got here. Still, it was a hard truth to swallow. She, Margie, and Jeanie had been so close these past few months. But it was her next thoughts that shocked her even more. "Jimmy, did you kill Kitty Cooper?"

"Had to," he replied.

"And you put something in Mister Sanders' dinner, didn't you? He died from some sort of poison."

"That should have gone undetected," he blurted out. "I discovered that he was writing a play for you and made the mistake of telling my sister. She started pressing me to get rid of you again, and I nearly agreed to it. It was obvious that he was trying to win your heart by writing an entire musical just for you."

"There was nothing between us, Jimmy," she told him.

"I realized that after you met with him at the restaurant. I could see that you didn't return his affections. So, I convinced my sister that stealing the manuscript from him would prevent you from starring in it. It was the only way to save you. And he needed to die slowly, for thinking that he had a chance with you. But that's not what I want to talk to you about. I want to discuss Jax Diamond."

She ignored him as another realization struck her, and she

could barely get the words out. "Oh, Jimmy. Did you kill Mister Beacham?"

He jumped to his feet. "I didn't want to. He was a nice old man, and I had nothing against him. But after I carried a crate into the music room for him, I saw his copy of Sam Sanders' manuscript. I had to take it from him. That was the deal between my sister and me. Mister Beacham caught me in the act. He asked why I was taking it, and I couldn't think of a good excuse. I knew then that he'd guessed I had something to do with Sam Sanders' death. I couldn't let him go to the police."

Laura fell silent now, thinking about how Mister Beacham had suffered. Probably right here in this room before Jimmy killed him and put him in the pond. She was sure that she was in one of the storage rooms at the theater now since Jimmy was one of the few people who had a key.

His previous comment entered her mind. He wanted to talk about Jax, and she knew why now, after what'd said about Mister Sanders. He wanted to find out how she felt about Jax, and she needed to avoid that conversation above all else. If he knew the truth, it would make the situation even worse for her. And put Jax in danger, too.

"You planted Mister Sander's ring in Robert Ashworth's desk, didn't you?" she asked as a distraction. "That's what convinced the police that he was guilty."

He sat down again. "I found something very interesting in Mister Ashworth's desk, Laura. I've been anxious to tell you about it. I think it will bring the two of us closer together. I can even help you deal with it. That's all I've ever wanted. To be closer to you."

As he spoke, she noticed that he had lowered the knife, and he appeared more relaxed. If she could keep him talking, she might be able to preoccupy him long enough to grab the keys and make an escape. It was a long shot, perhaps, but it was her only chance. "What did you find, Jimmy?"

"There was a document in his desk about your father."

She snapped out of her thoughts and stared at him. "What

about him?"

"Are you sure his death was an accident?"

Angrily, she got up and walked to the back of the room to put as much space between him and her. Jimmy was a killer, she reminded herself. A murderer. He would say anything to get under her skin right now, and she shouldn't listen to any of it. The situation was far too critical for her to get caught up in the past.

But the mere mention of her beloved father's death instantly broke through the barrier, the one she'd built to prevent herself from remembering. She was only eleven years old when she had watched her father's car burst into flames. And with no other reason given to the family except, the engine had overheated. With her father's knowledge of cars, his ability to build one from scratch, and ten years' experience racing them, it never made any sense to her.

"What did the document say?" she asked.

He suddenly charged towards her like a madman, backing her against the wall. "I want to talk about Jax Diamond first! I not only saved your life, but I even defied my sister by forging a letter to the director, instructing him to hire you to replace Kitty Cooper. My sister would be furious with me if she knew. She wanted that part more than anything in the world. Now tell me about Jax Diamond!"

"I don't know what you mean," she replied nervously. He stood no more than a foot away from her now, pointing the knife at her. "He...he's just some two-bit private detective who was..."

"Was what?" he shouted.

She struggled to think of what to say and how to say it so he couldn't tell that she was lying. "I didn't want to stay at his apartment. I loathe the man. But he...he forced me into it in hopes of catching the killer. He was using me, Jimmy." She caught a deep breath, praying she'd pacified him.

"So, he means nothing to you."

"No." But she'd hesitated for just a second and right off, she knew he didn't believe her.

"Sit down, Laura."

"Jimmy, listen to me."

"I said, sit down!"

She slid to the floor, still staring at the knife. He grabbed the satchel he'd brought with him and took out a coil of rope. He tied her hands together, then her ankles. All the while, she tried to convince him that Jax meant nothing to her. She even took it as far as to soothe him by saying that she's always been attracted to him, ever since she first met him in January when he helped out at the Imperial Theater during the Follies.

Yet, as though he were driven by some diabolical being, he finished securing her. Then, he pulled out a vine of berries from the satchel, and no matter how much she struggled and screamed, he shoved the poison down her throat.

"I know you weren't telling me the truth," he growled at her. "You're in love with him, not me. I heard it in your voice. I saw it on your face and in your eyes. And now, he has to die, too." And he stormed out of the room, locking it behind him.

28
Time's Ticking

Sunday, 3:30 a.m.

"Lucky for us, Mister Kratz agreed to go to the theater to get Jimmy's address for us," Tim said as he, Jax, and Ace hurried up the stairs to the top floor of the man's apartment building. "If Laura isn't here, remember that you both need to control your tempers. Don't kill Jimmy before he tells us where she is."

"That won't be easy for either of us," Jax stated.

When they stood in front of the door, Jax pounded on it, but no one answered. He glanced over at Tim, then kicked the door open. Tim just shook his head as they rushed inside and quickly started searching each room. Finally, Jax saw Ace by the back door and swung it open. They both began looking in every nook and crevice of the rooftop, then ended up standing in front of the makeshift greenhouse of plants. Jax pulled the canvas covering off of the support poles, and the moonlight shined on dozens of potted plants in every shape and size.

"I'm guessing these aren't just for decoration," Jax told Tim, who was standing in the doorway.

"Look what I found, Jax. Sanders' and Beacham's copies of the Songbird manuscript."

Jax brushed by him and went back into the apartment.

"Well, there's our proof. Now, we need to figure out where the heck he's got Laura."

"He's pretty clever, I'll give him that," Tim said. "He had everything he needed at his disposal by working at the theater. He even lives right around the corner from it."

Jax froze. "Murph, stay here in case Jimmy comes back. Ace and I are going to the theater. Hopefully, Mister Kratz is still there, and he can let me in. I have an idea."

But Ace started snarling.

Jax glimpsed Jimmy in the hallway and ran after him. "Stay back, Ace!" He knew Ace would kill the man if he caught Laura's scent on him.

At the top of the stairs, Jimmy stopped. He dropped his satchel, pulled out his knife, and flashed it at him. "It's too late to save her, Jax."

He darted towards Jimmy and tried knocking the weapon out of his hand. That failed, but he'd managed to wrap his other arm around the man's neck. While he held him there, shouting for him to tell him where Laura was, Jimmy drove the blade into his thigh. Jax winced with pain, and blood oozed through his trousers.

Ace barked ferociously and leaped forward.

"Get back, Ace!" Jax yelled. He shoved Jimmy against the wall, and the two of them wrestled for the knife.

Jax knew that he had greater strength, height, and determination, yet he was startled by Jimmy's tenacity. They fought so fiercely, both of them were knocked to the ground. Then, they tried to pin the other one down. Jax's arms were bleeding from Jimmy swiping the knife at him every chance he got. He finally caught ahold of his wrist, but Jimmy punched him directly into the wound in his thigh, and he lost his grip.

Jimmy wrapped both of his hands around the handle of the knife, lifted it over his head intending to thrust it deep into Jax's chest.

Tim called Ace off and pulled the trigger of his gun.

The bullet struck Jimmy in the back. The knife fell out of his hands, and he dropped to the floor.

"Jax, are you all right?" Tim asked as he rushed over.

"Yeah."

Tim quickly hovered over the other man's body to feel for a pulse. "Sorry, Jax. I didn't want to kill him, but I had no choice."

While Jax got to his feet, Tim grabbed the satchel and dumped everything out, hoping to find some clue as to Laura's whereabouts. A brass key ring jingled as it dropped to the floor. The noise grabbed their attention, but then, they both glared at the plant vine beside it. It had fallen out of the small paper bag lying there.

"Is that one of his poisonous plants?" Tim asked. "What do we do now?"

Jax bent down and grabbed the keys. "We pray to God that Laura is in the basement at the theater, and we're not too late. Bring that plant with us, Murph, but don't touch it with your hands."

Tim pointed to Jimmy. "What about *him*?"

"He's not going anywhere."

The theater was only three blocks away. When they got there, Jax and Ace jumped out of the car without waiting for Tim. Jax favored leg as they raced down the alley to the side door. He discovered it was open and burst inside. The only way to the basement that he knew of was from the second floor near Robert Ashworth's office. He headed up the steps to the main level, then caught himself.

Just in front of an open doorway, he saw Mister Kratz in a half-sitting position against the wall. He ran over to him and saw he was bleeding. "What happened?"

"I heard a noise coming from the back stairwell," he replied, holding his left side. "Jimmy Simmons attacked me with a knife."

Tim joined them. "I'll get an ambulance down here."

"Mister Kratz, do you know where Laura is?" Jax asked.

He looked puzzled. "Laura? No."

Jax looked over at the open door. "Do those stairs go to

the basement?" When Mister Kratz nodded, he turned to Tim. "Murph, call Doctor Norris and tell him to meet us at the hospital right away. Laura's got to be in one of the storage rooms down in the basement." He and Ace rushed down the stairwell, and they came to the maze of corridors. He knew there were dozens of storage rooms, and they didn't have time to search each one. "Ace, find Laura!"

Ace took off down the hall, and Jax ran after him, trying his best to keep up. They made so many left and right turns, he couldn't keep track of the pattern. He followed Ace down another hallway and saw a door at the end of it.

Frantically, Jax tried every key on the chain. One after another. Nervously, he shuffled through them, cursing to himself. But the next key easily slid into the lock. He yelled for Laura as soon as the door opened. It was too dark to see anything, so he followed Ace into the room.

"Jax! I'm over here," Laura cried as Ace licked her face. "Good boy, Ace."

Jax quickly untied her and lifted her into his arms.

"Jimmy forced me to eat some berries," Laura told him. "I spit out what I could after he left, but I'm not feeling very well, and I'm afraid..."

"It's okay, Laura, don't worry. I'll get you to the hospital." Jax followed Ace through the rest of the hallways, knowing that he would find the fastest way out of there.

"It was Jimmy who sent those gardenias to me, Jax," Laura whispered. "I tried to convince him that I didn't care what happened to you, but he could tell I was lying. He said he was going to kill you too. I was so scared that he would."

He kissed her forehead. "Shh. Don't talk, Laura. Save your strength. Doctor Norris is going to meet us at the hospital. He'll know what to do."

"Oh, Jax, your arm is bleeding."

"I know, sweetheart. I'm okay. Now please, stop talking."

Ace led them to the stairway on the opposite side of the theater, and they hurried to the car. After Jax carefully placed Laura in the passenger seat, he jumped in and pushed Old Nellie to her limits as they sped away. Thankfully, it was early in the morning, and very little traffic was on the road.

When they arrived at the hospital, he carried her inside, shouting for someone to help them. A few nurses hurried over with a gurney. He explained who he was, and they told him that Doctor Norris had already arrived and was waiting for them. He stayed by Laura's side, holding her hand tightly as they pushed her through the hall.

"Don't leave me, Jax," she said when they entered one of the rooms.

"Never," he told her. Doctor Norris hurried over to them. "She said that she ate some sort of berries," Jax explained. "I don't know what kind, but Sergeant Murphy is on his way with the plant vine we found."

"He mentioned as much when we spoke on the telephone," Doctor Norris replied. "I mixed up a strong concoction of crushed charcoal and several other herbs that hopefully will absorb whatever she consumed." He went over to the counter, picked up a large coffee mug, and approached Laura. "Miss Graystone, I need you to drink this down. All of it. And as quickly as possible. It tastes wretched, so I mixed it with some sweet juice."

"My mouth is so parched right now, I'm willing to drink anything." She took the mug, looked at Jax, and tried to smile. "Bottom's up."

Jax forced a grin while stroking her hair.

Doctor Norris took the mug from her when she was done. "As soon as Sergeant Murphy arrives, I will find out exactly what you ingested, Laura. It is best if you try to remain quiet and even sleep if you can."

"Thank you, Doctor."

Jax took a deep breath. "I can't tell you how much we appreciate you getting here as quick as you did, Doctor Norris."

"I would like to speak with you for a moment in private if you don't mind," he said.

Jax frowned with the request, but he turned a smile on

Laura. "I'll be right back. I promise." She nodded, so he followed the doctor into the hall. "She seems lucid right now, Doctor, so maybe it wasn't enough to harm her?"

"Some toxins take longer than others to enter a person's entire system. It all depends upon what type of berries they were, and how much she ingested. I cannot guarantee this will work. I put a teaspoon of activated charcoal in her drink. The efficacy of charcoal also depends upon how quickly it is administered. Do you know how long it has been since she ate the berries?"

Jax was overwrought and tried to think. "We've been searching for her since a little after six o'clock last night. It would've taken some time to get her out of Grand Central to the theater. And I'm pretty sure the person responsible didn't give them to her right way." He was thinking about Jimmy and his affection for Laura. It would have taken quite a while before he became angry enough to kill her. "The man is dead, so I can't say for sure."

"Well then, time will tell. All we can do is hope for the best."

"When will we know for sure?"

"The next twelve hours will be critical," Doctor Norris stated.

Jax tried to his emotions in check. "Is there anything else we can do? She means the world to me, Doctor Norris."

"I can see that, Jax. She is a beautiful young woman, strong and healthy from what I can see."

He let out a sad chuckle. "You don't know the half of it. She's the strongest woman I've ever known."

"Then, she probably has a good chance. Looks like you got into a little bit of a scrape. I'll send a nurse in to patch you up. I will be close by in case you need me."

Jax thanked him and went back into the room. Laura had closed her eyes, so he pulled a chair over and sat there, gazing at her.

After a few minutes, Tim entered the room. "Ace was waiting by the door out front, and I couldn't leave him there," he whispered as Ace went over to sit beside Jax. "I'll tell the nurses that he's on duty. I gave the vine to Doctor Norris."

"He said it could be several hours before we know anything. You've been up all night, too, Murph. Why don't you go home to your family?"

"Not a chance, partner. Carla is dropping the kids off with her parents. She wants to be here, too, if that's okay."

"It sure is. We could use all the prayers we can get." He looked over at Laura. "It's my fault he forced her to eat those berries. She said she tried to convince Jimmy that she didn't care about me, but he didn't believe her."

Tim grew angry. "Why are you always blaming yourself for everything? This is all Jimmy's fault and that devil sister of his. Besides, Laura couldn't convince him because she loves you just as much as you love her, Jax."

He nodded. "Thanks, Murph." And the three of them waited there quietly.

29
Duet

Sunday, 5:00 p.m.

Jax and Ace sat stiff and alert still watching Laura. Neither of them had moved a muscle in the past twelve hours, except for the two times Doctor Norris, another doctor and three nurses asked them to leave the room. Laura now lay there with a nasal oxygen catheter, although Doctor Norris explained it had been administered simply as a precaution.

Jax had insisted Tim and Carla go home to their kids after promising that he would call them with any news. Then, he sat there motionless and numb. It seemed as though every emotion had shut down as he watched Laura drift in and out of consciousness during those hours. The only thing on his mind was how quickly she had tripped into his life and his heart. She was an amazing woman, and he couldn't bear the thought of losing her now.

After two more hours had passed, Jax leaned forward and

held his head in his hands. Ace pawed at his leg then stuck his nose through to lay his snout on the crook of his arm.

But Jax heard Laura stirring. He got to his feet and stood beside her. She looked over at him and quietly whispered his name. "I'm right here, Laura. I told you that I wouldn't leave you." He gazed into her eyes and noticed they looked much clearer. "How are you feeling?"

"Achy and sore, like a brick wall fell over me. A little lightheaded, too." She smiled at him as he brushed tendrils of hair off her forehead. "And I'm really hungry."

He laughed, and a tear fell down his cheeks. "I'll buy you to whatever you want."

Ace lifted his front paws onto the bed, and Laura petted him. "You're my hero, Ace. You are, too, Jax. I wouldn't have made it if it weren't for both of you."

"Let me get Doctor Norris to check on you," Jax told her. "I'm going to give that man a great big hug." He hurried out of the room, thanking God as he went.

Doctor Norris and few nurses hurried into the room. Jax stepped aside and listened to them converse with her while they removed the oxygen tube. The Doctor finally turned to him. "I'd like to keep her here another day or two, but she's going to be fine."

Jax grabbed the man's hand and shook it furiously in gratitude. The Doctor patted him on the shoulder and left the room. One of the nurses agreed to call Tim to let him know, and Jax went back to be with Laura. And he stayed with her that night. They talked for a while, and when she finally fell asleep, he slid back in the chair and slept like a baby.

Friday, June 15

Laura was released from the hospital on Wednesday with a clean bill of health, and she moved back into her own apartment. Jax had explained to her that Jimmy was dead, and he'd told her that Margie was going to be in jail for a very long time. And they were both relieved that neither of them would hurt anyone else again.

"It was so kind of Joe Marsh to move Mister Beacham's funeral to this afternoon," Laura said as she and Jax left his apartment.

"There wouldn't be one without you," Jax told her. He locked his door, and they walked down the hall.

One of the other tenants headed towards them. A beautiful, tall blonde woman. "Hello, Jax," she said sweetly.

"How are you, Lucinda?" Jax replied.

Laura narrowed her eyes and glared at him as they walked down the stairs. "Isn't that funny? She has the same name as your sister."

He chuckled uneasily. "Yeah, must be a popular name."

For a split second, she considered telling him that she knew the truth about his family. But she decided against it. She'd promised Tim that she wouldn't say anything, and she thought it would be best for Jax to tell her when he was ready.

Instead, she laughed and wrapped her arm in his as they walked to his car. "I received a phone call from Ben Hoffman this morning. He said that he owns the rights to the Songbird manuscript, and he offered me the lead."

Jax didn't respond right away. "Well, that would definitely make you a Broadway star for sure. It's your dream come true, isn't it?"

"Yes, but that play has caused so much heartache. Mister Hoffman said production wouldn't start until fall, so I have time to think about it."

He remained silent.

"There's something else that's troubling me, Jax. I've tried not to think about what happened last weekend, but Jimmy told me something very strange when we were in the storage room. At the time, I got pretty upset hearing about it, but the rest happened and I put it out of my mind."

"I wouldn't trust anything he said."

"I know, but it had to do with my father. He said that he found some sort of document in Robert Ashworth's desk. Then, he asked me if my father's death was an accident."

"All I saw in that drawer was a pile of financial records. Ralph Boyer, the city's accountant, took a closer look at them. I don't think he found anything other than evidence of Ashworth's money laundering scheme."

"Even so, I wondered if we could take a look at those files? Like you said, Jimmy couldn't be trusted, but I'm still curious."

"I'll talk to Ralph Boyer about it."

"Thank you. There's one more thing. I've also decided to go home to Millbury for a few weeks. I miss my mother and brother and after what happened, I need some time away from all the glitter and lights."

Jax just nodded.

When they arrived at the cemetery, they were both surprised to see the large crowd that had gathered for the funeral. Tim, Carla, Jeanie, and all the performers and stagehands who had worked with Mister Beacham attended, along with several of the officers from the thirteenth precinct. The minister gave a beautiful sermon, with several people offering to share their warm and loving memories of Horace Beacham. Afterward, as everyone headed for their vehicles, a few people stopped to ask Jax for directions to the funeral reception.

Laura was confused. "What reception?"

He wrapped his arm around her. "I planned a very special musical send-off for your friend, and I asked everyone to join us." She looked up at him curiously, and he flashed that dimpled grin at her. "I reserved Duke's Club for the rest of the afternoon. You and I have some entertaining to do."

"Oh, Jax, what a wonderful idea."

As they drove to the north end of Manhattan, Laura couldn't keep her eyes off him. She had never known anyone like Jax before. He was as handsome as he was corny and clever. And surprisingly smart and thoughtful. When he glanced over at her, she didn't turn away as she'd done before, afraid that he would see how she truly felt about him. She simply smiled in return and continued watching him.

They arrived at Duke's Club, and it was swarming with all the same people who had attended the funeral. The band was on stage, already playing tunes for everyone to enjoy. As they made their way to one of the front tables, they greeted and thanked everyone for coming. Then, they sat down to enjoy the music.

"Jax, this is the perfect tribute to Mister Beacham," she told him. "He would have loved it."

"Oh, there's more to come, Laura." Jax waited until the band stopped playing, then he stood up. "Don't go anywhere." He winked at her and joined the others on stage. But instead of retrieving his trumpet, he walked over to the microphone and waited until the room was quiet.

"Thank you all for coming here today to honor Horace Beacham," he announced. "I didn't know the man personally, but it's obvious that he had a lot of friends who cared about him. I thought it would be very fitting for Laura to sing a special song for him today." And he motioned for her to come up on stage with him.

Everyone started clapping. She was in disbelief and nearly in tears. But she stood up and joined him. "Why didn't you tell me?" she whispered to him.

"Sing *April Showers*, Laura. You know the tune. I'll accompany you on the piano in his stead."

"You play the piano?"

He shrugged his shoulders and handed her the microphone.

She watched him in amazement as he sat behind the piano. As soon as he began playing, she chimed in, singing the beautiful song that was so perfect for the occasion. Slowly, she wandered over to be closer to Jax, keeping her eyes on his.

As soon as the tune ended, Jax got up and made his way over to her. He snatched her hand and pulled her into his arms in front of everyone. He gazed at her and ran the back of his fingers gently over her cheek.

She smiled at him. "You told me that you were out of surprises."

"I have a few more up my sleeve," he whispered. "Tell your mother to ready the couch. Ace and I are going to Millbury with you. I need a break from the glitter and lights, too, Laura. And I never want to lose you."

He leaned down and kissed her with every passion in his heart. She wrapped her arms around his neck and pulled him closer. And the crowd stood up and cheered.

The End

(That is, until the next book releases in early Spring, 2022)

A SPECIAL NOTE TO READERS

https://www.gailmeath.com

Thank you very much for reading *Songbird*. I hope you enjoyed it. Usually, I write historical romance novels based upon the lives of heroic women and events in history. Originally, I intended this book to be based upon the true *Broadway Butterfly Murders* that took place in New York City in 1923-24.

Dorothy King and Louise Lawson were two not-so-famous actresses who were drawn away from their Broadway careers by a few wealthy businessmen who showered them with furs and diamonds. They were both killed separately a year apart, and their murders remain unsolved to this day. Back then, the newspaper headlines had read, "Who Killed the Broadway Butterflies?"

Yet, as I continued writing and researching the era, I had so much fun learning about the way of life on Broadway during the Roaring Twenties before the depression, my story ended up more lighthearted than I had expected, and it merely includes some fictionalized tidbits addressing the murders.

During my research, I happened upon a couple great videos that I wanted to share with you. The first one is a live video of Coney Island in the 1920s. What a hoot! The rides were none too safe back then! The second video is Judy Garland singing her 1959 rendition of *April Showers*, which was one of the most popular songs in 1923. And the last video is a taste of the jazz era that rocked and altered the music world forever in so many ways.

Canned Thrills at Coney Island in the 1920s
https://www.youtube.com/watch?v=9Wz5vZmU8Dc&t=47s
(Dusty Old Thing, 2/19/2019)

Judy Garland sings "April Showers" finale from "GE Theatre" 1956
https://www.youtube.com/watch?v=zsfXi5BKkNo
(Entertainment Buff, 7/4/2011)

Original Memphis Five - Tin Roof Blues 1923
https://www.youtube.com/watch?v=43S1Yk5PMoU
(Bsgs98, 4/11/2012)

Thank you again for your time and interest! If you enjoyed *Songbird*, I hope you will take a moment to leave a review at your favorite retailer. I would greatly appreciate it! And please feel free to contact me on my website, Facebook page or by email at, gailmeathauthor@gmail.com.

All my best, Gail

HISTORICAL ROMANCE COLLECTION

AGUSTINA DE ARAGON (1803)
A true Spanish heroine during Napoleon War

COUNTESS JACQUELINE (1413)
Medieval based upon a True Story

FIRE BLOSSOM (1843)
Western in Texas

THE PERFECT SISTER (1904)
Murder-Mystery in New York

HOLBROOK MANOR (1910)
Western Murder-Mystery

PATH OF TREASURES (1852)
Murder-Mystery on the Erie Canal

FATEFUL STRANGERS (1785)
High-Seas Adventure

SCANDAL IN BOSTON (1848)
Murder-Mystery in Boston

Printed in Great Britain
by Amazon